A SHOCKING PLAN

Sarah sat perched in the tree in the moonlight as Margaret and John stopped beneath it. They spoke quietly, but she could hear them. She wondered if she should let them know she was there, but she thought how foolish she would feel.

"Surely there's an unmarried woman in the settlement you care for, John," Margaret said. She was silent for a moment, then quietly said words that made Sarah's icy cheeks burn.

"Sarah will be sixteen in March. She's of an age to marry."

A cry of disbelief sprang to Sarah's lips, but she managed to stifle it, and pressed her cheek hard against the tree. Of an age to marry? She, Sarah? Her brain pounded against her skull as though wanting to be free. She clutched the tree harder for fear she would faint and plummet to the ground. Marry, and be tied to Virginia forever? *Never!* she wanted to scream at the figures below. *Never!*

SARAH
ON HER
OWN

KAREN M. COOMBS

AN AVON FLARE BOOK

SARAH ON HER OWN is an original publication of Avon Books. This work has never before appeared in book form.

AVON BOOKS
A division of
The Hearst Corporation
1350 Avenue of the Americas
New York, New York 10019

Copyright © 1996 by Karen Mueller Coombs
Map courtesy of Virginia Norey
Excerpt from *Plainsong for Caitlin* copyright © 1996 by Elizabeth Marraffino
Published by arrangement with the author
Library of Congress Catalog Card Number: 95-94934
ISBN: 0-380-78275-8
RL: 6.1

First Avon Flare Printing: March 1996

AVON FLARE TRADEMARK REG. U.S. PAT. OFF. AND IN OTHER COUNTRIES, MARCA REGISTRADA, HECHO EN U.S.A.

Printed in the U.S.A.

RA   10   9   8   7   6   5   4   3   2   1

To the memory of my grandparents, Howard and Jennie Bellamy, who believed ...

With thanks to my writing support groups, past and present; and to L.Z., for her helpful suggestions

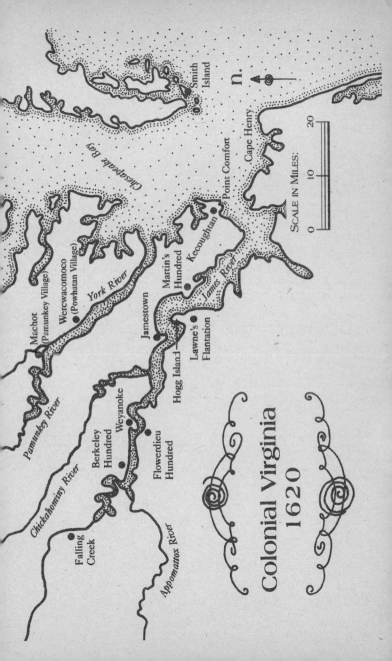

Colonial Virginia
1620

SCALE IN MILES:
0   10   20

n.

Smith Island

Chesapeake Bay

Cape Henry

Point Comfort

Kecoughan

Martin's Hundred

York River

Werowocomoco
(Powhatan Village)

Machot
(Pamunkey Village)

Jamestown

Lawne's
Plantation

Hogg Island

Pamunkey River

Weyanoke

Berkeley Hundred

Flowerdieu Hundred

Chickahominy River

Falling Creek

Appomattox River

James River

Prologue

In the 1600s, the English poet Drayton called Virginia "Earth's only Paradise." The English had many hopes for this paradise, most of them false. They thought gold lay upon the ground for the picking. They thought they would find a new passage to India if they searched long enough. By settling Virginia they hoped to keep the land out of Spanish hands and to gain more followers for the Protestant Church by converting the Indians.

In 1606, James I, King of England, granted a charter to the Virginia Company of London, giving it the right to establish permanent settlements in Virginia. The Company raised money for settlements by selling shares to private investors and to smaller joint-stock companies, which were then entitled to share in any profits returned from the new colony.

Those settlers who traveled to Virginia, however, were lucky to survive, much less send profits back to the Virginia Company in England, and there was no money to share with the Company's investors. Instead, the Company offered investors tracts of Virginia land large enough to support one hundred families. These became known as "hundreds."

One of these tracts was granted to the Martin's Hundred Society, named after its largest investor, Richard Martin. The first settlement was founded in Martin's Hundred in 1619, when two hundred people established a community called Wolstenholme Towne, named after another Martin's Hundred investor, Sir John Wolstenholme.

Approximately 3,560 people traveled to Martin's Hundred between 1619 and 1621. They were not hoping to find gold, or a passage to India, or new church converts. Planters went hoping to find rich land. Women went hoping to find husbands. Servants went hoping to find freedom. All found hunger and disease. Three thousand found death.

Sarah Douglas sailed to Virginia in 1620. This is the story of what she found.

Chapter 1

During the night, the Atlantic storm that had raged for four days and nights waned, the groans and creaks of the ship's timbers eased, and the *Jonathan* began to ride more peacefully. The change woke fourteen-year-old Sarah Douglas. She raised herself on one elbow, pulling her skirts away from the seawater that trickled across the planking near her pallet.

Candles guttered in the few lanterns and cast a dim light on the other women passengers in the shadowy hold. They slumped among their belongings, crouched retching into buckets, or lay moaning with the fever that had pounced on them only days before. A few lucky ones slept.

"Aaahhh!" Sarah cried softly, when she spied a large rat nosing around Aunt Mary, who slept beside her. Too tired to eat, Aunt Mary had wrapped a moldy ship's biscuit in a handkerchief and tucked it under her head. The rat, grown bold in the cramped quarters of the ship, was after the biscuit.

Her hand trembling, Sarah reached down and seized her shoe. "Scat!" she whispered, waving the shoe and hoping the rat would scamper off.

The rat simply bared its teeth and continued snuffling

around Aunt Mary's head. Remembering the bite marks she had seen on the neck of one woman who had died, Sarah hesitantly poked the toe of her shoe at the rat's hind end.

"Ssst! Ssst!" she hissed. Finally, holding her breath, Sarah sat up and smacked the shoe down on the end of the creature's tail. With a nasty squeak, it was gone.

The noise woke her friend Anne Bell, lying on the other side of Sarah. "Rat," Sarah whispered. "And Anne, the storm's ending. We won't have to be shut below decks in this heat much longer."

Anne smiled. "I'll miss the smell of vomit and un-washed bodies," she joked, sitting up and wrapping her arms around her knees, her copper-colored hair the only bright spot in the gloom.

Sarah leaned back against the side of the ship. "I won't miss it," she said. "And neither will you." There were nearly two hundred passengers aboard the *Jonathan*, most of them women. Sarah had counted nearly one hundred and fifty shut below deck. Many were ill. Some had died. During the days the ship was buffeted like a twig caught in a millrace, the dead had been shoved through the wooden porthole into the raging sea, without even the proper words said over their wasted bodies.

Sarah sighed, rubbing her hands over her cheeks. "It's a while till morning, but I'll never get back to sleep again."

"Nor will I," Anne whispered. In the six weeks they'd been aboard, neither girl had slept more than a few hours at a time. "You can't sleep when lice are chewing on you," Anne added, scratching at her shoulder.

Or when you're furious and fearful, Sarah thought. She frowned at Aunt Mary's huddled form as fluttering shadows wavered over the sleeping woman. *Oh, how I wish you'd never met Charles,* she silently told her aunt. Aunt Mary answered with a raspy snore, then restlessly rolled onto her back.

It was unusual for Aunt Mary to toss about, and Sarah stared at her, her stomach trembling at the sight of Mary's flushed face, the dark hollows under her eyes. She touched her aunt's forehead with the back of her fingers, then turned to Anne and clutched her sleeve.

"God, help us. Aunt Mary has the fever," she told her friend.

Anne quickly crawled around Sarah to kneel beside the woman. "Wet a cloth," she ordered.

Her heart churning, Sarah quickly rose and dipped a rag into the barrel of filthy water nearby. She watched as Anne wiped Aunt Mary's face and picked off all the lice she could find, popping them angrily on her fingernail. Then Sarah and Anne wrapped both their rugs around her.

Please, don't die, Sarah silently begged her sleeping aunt. *I'll stop being angry with you. I'll try to like Virginia. Just don't die. You're all I have left in the world.* Her aunt's only answer was a moan.

A few hours later, Aunt Mary, her brow dotted with beads of sweat, opened her eyes and looked at Sarah. "Catherine," she said, smiling a wretched smile. "Out. Garden. Cooler there. House . . . so warm . . . time of year."

"She thinks I'm my mother," Sarah whispered to Anne.

"It's the fever," Anne told her.

When Sarah was eight, her mother had died in childbirth, so Sarah's father James had asked his sister Mary to come and live with them. Though only ten years older than Sarah, Mary was like a mother to her.

Anne held a piggin of the ship's thick, brackish water to Aunt Mary's cracked lips, but the liquid only dribbled down her chin. "If only there were some beer or stout ale left," she told Sarah.

"It wouldn't be fit to drink if there were." Sarah was unable to keep the bitterness from her voice. She started to wind a strand of her wavy hair round and round her finger until her finger disappeared under a crinkly, brown cocoon. "The drink was sour before it ran dry two weeks ago. Stinking, like everything else on this ship."

Anne set down the water and put an arm around Sarah's shoulders. "Hush," she said. "Think of something else, something pleasant. Tell me about your Aunt Mary."

Sarah sighed, thankful she and Anne had become friends soon after the *Jonathan* sailed down the Thames from London. Though younger, Sarah felt she had known the seventeen-year-old Anne forever. She sighed again, Anne's arm around her a tiny comfort in the midst of misery.

"I've told you all there is to tell."

"Tell me again," insisted Anne.

"Aunt Mary refused a marriage proposal to care for me and Father," Sarah began, fanning herself with a soft, slender hand marred by bitten nails.

"Knowing you, I suspect marriage would have been an easier undertaking," Anne teased, tucking a loose corner of rug around Aunt Mary.

"I suppose I was a bit of a rascal," Sarah agreed. "But I think Father was even more of a trial to her. He made very little money, you know. And most of it he spent on books for the two of us to share. Aunt Mary worried that we'd all starve."

"You did well enough." Anne poked herself, then Sarah, gently in the ribs. "Though not as sturdy as I, you're almost as tall."

"Thanks to Aunt Mary's skill with the needle, we

usually ate well enough." Sarah looked down at her lean body and sighed. "That's how she met Charles, you know. She sewed him a pair of breeches." She bit the back of her hand, as though to hold in the anger trying to spew out. "Oh, how I wish she'd never met him and we'd never heard of that cursed Virginia!" Sniffling, she wiped the back of her hand across her nose. Her nose, inherited from her father, was the one thing Sarah truly disliked about her looks. She thought it was too straight and long, and hated its few scattered freckles. As a child, she had constantly pressed on the end of it, hoping to halt its growth.

"Aunt Mary taught me to sew a bit, you know. She said I might be good enough to open my own shop someday. But what good is a fine shop in the New World? What shall I sew? Animal skins?" She began to laugh, quietly at first, then louder. There was no joy in the sound, only pain. "Animal skins?" she asked again, her voice breaking. She nodded her head, as though in greeting. "Good morning, madam, may I interest you in a fine gown with an underskirt of squirrel? A bodice of wolf? Sleeves made from the softest . . . ?"

"Hush!" Anne ordered, her large blue eyes brimming with tears. "What if your aunt can hear you?"

Sarah shuddered and was quiet. "I know it's selfish, and I shouldn't be thinking about my own troubles when my dear aunt lies ill," she said then, "but I can't help wishing Aunt Mary had refused to marry Charles, just as she refused her first proposal. Or that she had at least left me behind."

"And with your father dead and your aunt gone off, what would you have done? How would you have lived? You're scarcely out of your childhood." Anne gently brushed a damp corkscrew of brown hair off Sarah's forehead.

"I could have apprenticed myself to a seamstress,"

Sarah said. "Yes, I'd have been alone, but at least it would have been in a familiar place, not in some savage new land where I'll likely starve to death or get murdered by a heathen—if living on this squalid ship doesn't kill me first." She would have said more, but at that moment Aunt Mary opened her eyes and peered at Sarah as though looking through a thick mist. Her eyes glittered, huge in her sunken face.

"Sarah," she whispered.

Relief caught at Sarah's throat, turning her bones to water. Her aunt recognized her. "Listen, Aunt Mary," Sarah said. "The storm has ended. Soon we'll go up on deck again. You'll feel better with the touch of sea air upon your cheek. We all will."

Aunt Mary feebly waved aside her words. "Sarah," she said, ". . . won't see . . . Virginia." She held up a hand as though to halt any protest.

But Sarah sat mute. No words could pass the huge, beating lump of despair that had suddenly grown at the base of her throat.

Aunt Mary rested a moment. Then, her voice a whisper Sarah could scarcely hear, said, "Charles. Tell . . . love him. Love you." Her eyes closed, but she continued. "I know you . . . dread Virginia. But new land. New life. New hope. Don't be afraid, for 'He shall give his angels . . . charge over thee, to . . . keep thee in all thy . . . ways.' Live well, dear Sarah. Live well." Aunt Mary sighed and was silent.

Then Sarah's words came. "Charles will be at Jamestown to meet us," she prattled, although these were not the words she wanted to speak. She wanted to tell her aunt how much she dreaded the New World, how angry she was that Aunt Mary was taking her there, how terrified she was that her aunt might die and leave her to face Virginia alone. But those words would have caused her aunt great distress. So instead, Sarah said what her

8

aunt would want to hear. The girl's only thought was that if she kept talking, Aunt Mary would have to listen. And if she were listening, she couldn't die.

"You and Charles will be married, and the three of us will live a wonderful life. You'll see. Soon you'll have children of your own. I'd love to have cousins. Then, when I'm a few years older . . ."

Anne touched Sarah's wrist. Only then did Sarah realize she had been squeezing Aunt Mary's hands as though she could keep her in this world.

Aunt Mary tried to smile, but it was like a grimace. Her head fell back, and she was again in a stupor, her breath thick and choking.

Sarah scarcely left Aunt Mary's side that long night. Later, when gray light of morning crept into the ship's hold, the dying woman began to rave. "Want out," she moaned, tossing on her pallet. "Want out. Door . . . closed. Please open the door so I may go out. Charles . . . waiting. Please open the door. I want to go out."

There was nothing Sarah could do. So, her body stiff, her heart trembling, she simply sat and gently held Aunt Mary's hand.

A short time later Sarah heard a scuffling overhead. The noise made Aunt Mary more restless. Then the hatch, which had been battened for so many days, was thrown open with a thud, and a shaft of daylight plunged into the dusk. The brightness made Sarah squint with pain before she glanced again at Aunt Mary.

Her aunt lay still, peering toward the light and smiling as at an old, familiar friend come to call. She reached up toward it. "At last," she sighed. "I've been waiting." Her arm dropped; a breath rattled out of her; her eyes glazed. She was dead.

Sarah reached out to touch Aunt Mary's cheek, then

drew back when Mary's voice echoed in her head: "Sarah Douglas, you really must stop gnawing on your fingernails. They look as though a beaver has dined on them." Then Aunt Mary's bubbling laugh swirled around Sarah before slowly rising with the dust motes toward the open hatch.

Sarah crossed her arms over her chest and tucked her hands with their ragged nails under them. Then, her head bowed, she began to rock.

Now that, when Mary's body settled in her bunk
South Carolina, probable, and I don't know what
that meant

Chapter 2

A few hours later Aunt Mary's shrouded body was
slipped over the side of the *Jonathan* and into
the sea. The sea air felt sweet upon Sarah's brow, and
she knew she should stay for the burial of the three
other women who had also died last night, but she had
no desire to remain where the other passengers could
see her drawn, grieving face, her reddened eyes. So she
eeled her way through the crowd surrounding Captain
Thompson to go below.

She was near the hatch when Lieutenant Richard
Kean stepped into her path. Lieutenant Kean was on his
way to Martin's Hundred, a plantation near Jamestown,
where he was to be in charge of defense. Since the
voyage began, Anne had been breathless over the mere
sight of the man, but his haughty manner made Sarah
quiver.

Richard Kean bowed, then put his hat back on his
head and said, "I am sorry about your aunt, Mistress
Douglas. Your loss must be a painful one."

Sarah fixed her eyes on one of Lieutenant Kean's
boots. "You're most kind," she mumbled.

As Lieutenant Kean touched his hat and turned to go,
Sarah was amazed that she had been able to speak to

the man. She'd had no brother, and for most of her life her father was the only man she knew. So usually, if a man spoke to her, her face flushed red and her tongue lay dead in her mouth. It had taken her nearly three months before she felt comfortable talking with Aunt Mary's Charles, and even then he always asked her to speak up and stop mumbling.

Only three words spoken, but spoken to Richard Kean himself, Sarah thought, as she climbed down the ladder, *and my tongue didn't trip over them. If only Anne had been with me. She has been wanting to speak with Richard Kean for nearly five weeks. I doubt she'd have let him walk away after only a snippet of conversation. And if he* had *tried to walk away, Anne probably would have flung her arms around his ankles,* Sarah decided, then scolded herself for thinking silly thoughts so soon after Aunt Mary's funeral.

It was so dreary below when Sarah reached the bottom of the ladder, she regretted leaving the fresh air. Then she thought how wonderful it would be to have a few moments of solitude, for there had been so little of it on the voyage. Muffled groans told her a few sick souls with no strength to climb the ladder still lay below, but a few didn't matter when there were usually so many.

As she neared her sleeping area, Sarah saw a figure bent over Aunt Mary's chest, pawing through her belongings. Rose Hawkings.

Something about Rose always raised the hair on Sarah's neck and made her feel like a timid mouse. Perhaps it was because Rose looked to be older even than Anne, someone who had lived a hard life. Now, though Sarah longed for enough courage to scream "Get away!" at Rose, she scarcely managed to whisper, "What are you doing?"

Rose dropped the shawl she was fingering and turned

to face Sarah. "Near put me in a fine froth, you did, creeping up on a body that way." She was smiling, but her eyes didn't meet Sarah's.

"What are you doing?" Sarah repeated, a bit more boldly.

"Just givin' you a hand, girlie, that's all." Rose's smile disappeared, and a hard look crept onto her face. She was pretty in a lean, hungry way, but her fierce look made Sarah think of a fox cornered in a henhouse.

"Law says sailors can help themselves to the goods of any passenger what up and dies aboard ship," Rose went on. "I was just gonna take a few of your dead aunt's things and hide 'em for you so's the sailors can't get 'em."

Liar, thought Sarah, wishing she had the courage to give Rose a clout on the head. "That was kind of you, Rose," she said, biting a thumbnail, "but I don't think the sailors can take anything if a relative of the dead person is on board."

She felt a movement at her shoulder. Anne slipped her arm through Sarah's. "Sarah's right," she said, then snapped, "And if I ever catch you ferreting around our belongings again, Rose Hawkings, I'll break your head."

Sarah squeezed Anne's arm with her own in silent gratitude, as Rose studied them from under her brows.

"No need to be so nasty to a body what's only doin' you a favor," snarled Rose. "But if that be the way you feel, I'll not be doin' you another." She gave Anne a sour look, picked up Aunt Mary's shawl and deliberately wiped her grimy hands on it before flinging it back into the chest and strutting away.

A week later, Sarah clambered up the ladder to the deck, as usual catching the toe of her shoe in her hem.

Anne was near the bow of the ship, leaning into the breeze, a blissful look on her face.

"Come stand beside me, Sarah," she called. "The sea air is so bracing.

"Thank goodness for May sunshine," she said when Sarah joined her at the rail. "I can imagine what the hopeful bridegrooms will think if we arrive in the New World looking like ghosts. But then, with so few women in Virginia, the lads might be happy to marry any woman, ghost *or* flesh." Anne giggled, then added wistfully, "Oh, I hope I find a good man to marry."

Anne and nearly one hundred other women on board had been recruited by the Virginia Company of London to go to Virginia to become wives to the unmarried colonists. Their fares would be paid by the men they married, but they wouldn't be forced to wed against their will. Anne had said that most of the courting and marrying would take place in the first few days ashore. Sarah couldn't imagine marrying at all, much less marrying a man she'd scarcely met. She marveled that Anne and the others could be so excited about it.

Sarah pulled Anne down beside her out of the wind. "Can you be happy married to a stranger?"

"Happier than I would have been if I'd married that Devon lout my father picked for me," Anne answered. "Besides, I intend to be very careful when choosing my husband." She sighed, and wrinkled her freckled nose. "If only Richard Kean would glance my way, I might beat all the other maids to the altar. I doubt there's a better man waiting in Virginia."

Sarah curled her lip. "Richard Kean's nose is so far in the air he can only glance heavenward."

"Oh, Sarah," Anne said with a laugh.

At that moment something pierced Sarah's scalp, and the hair on the back of her neck rose. "Anne, help! I feel a louse making a meal of me."

Anne's fingers deftly searched Sarah's scalp. "This task wouldn't be so tedious if the damp air didn't make your hair curl so," she complained. Finally, the vermin found, she popped the louse between her fingers. Then the girls began to pick through each other's hair for the foul pests and their nits. It was a nasty job, but one that would make them more comfortable.

They had been sitting there for some time, plucking and popping, when Sarah lifted her head to see Richard Kean standing against the rail midships. He had been staring at them, though when Sarah looked up he turned his eyes seaward.

"You have your wish," Sarah told Anne. "Richard Kean was just now looking our way."

"Goodness!" said Anne, blushing. "I'm so embarrassed. We should have found a more private place to pick our vermin."

"You think he has no lice in his cabin to make him miserable?"

Anne giggled, recovering her good humor. "Oh, I'm sure they're in his cabin, but I doubt even a louse would touch the body of Richard Kean without an invitation."

"Yes," agreed Sarah. "He seems so strong and sure of himself, he frightens me. I imagine a louse would feel the same."

"But don't you think he's handsome?" asked Anne.

The two girls sat peeping at the man from the corner of their eyes.

"He seems to be all juts and slopes," Sarah told Anne.

"But look how his hair—it's almost the same brown as yours, Sarah—curls back off his forehead so finely."

"But that forehead is pitched backward like a roof-top," Sarah protested. "His mustache curls upward as though trying to call attention to his jutting cheekbones, and his nose is flattened at the tip as though he spent his childhood with his face pressed against a mirror.''

"He has a fine cleft in his chin.''

"It was put there on purpose to divide his beard neatly in half,'' Sarah answered airily. "And while his nose is long and blunt, that beard is short and pointed.''

The girls' critical description of Lieutenant Kean amused them so much they broke into loud giggles. Then an abrupt wave of remorse stopped Sarah's laughter, and she covered her face with her hands. "I shouldn't be so merry while I'm still in mourning for my aunt,'' she muttered.

"Posh!'' said Anne. "Laughter brings a welcome light into your eyes. I hadn't noticed they had so much gray among the blue.'' She patted Sarah's hand. "Don't worry,'' she said. "Anyone who has ever suffered loss knows grief and joy are flip sides of the same pancake.''

"You always know what to say to make me feel better.'' Sarah peeked through her fingers at Richard Kean again. "You know, this is the first time I've really looked at Lieutenant Kean. When he's around, I'm so flustered I don't notice his appearance. His features taken alone are rather disjointed. But joined together on one face, they all seem to belong.'' She gave Anne a poke, and added in a teasing voice, "Maybe he is a little bit handsome.''

"Oh, he is,'' sighed Anne. "And the scar on his cheek makes him even more so. He no doubt got it fighting for the king.''

At that moment Richard Kean began to walk to where the girls sat crouched out of the wind. He carried his head high, and his nostrils flaring, seemed to sniff the wind like a wild pony on the moors. Sarah looked at Anne with dismay when he stopped beside them.

"Can you not smell it?'' he asked, looking down at them.

"Smell what, sir?" asked Anne.

"Up on your feet!" thundered Richard Kean.

The girls were so astonished by his command, they immediately leaped up, not even stopping to question his right to order them about. Placing his hands upon their shoulders, Kean spun them into the wind.

"Now do you smell it?" he asked, his voice low, yet so full of excitement it was clear he could scarcely control it.

Sarah breathed, pulling air deep into her chest, searching for the elusive odor Richard sensed upon the wind.

"I *can* smell it!" she cried at last.

"Oh, yes," echoed Anne. "I can smell it, too."

"And what do you smell, ladies?" This time Richard's voice didn't thunder.

Anne and Sarah answered as one. "Land! I smell land!"

Chapter 3

For the past few days gulls had been hovering around the ship, and the passengers had smelled the fresh breath of pine upon the wind from the west. Then the trees themselves loomed on the horizon, appearing to rise directly from the waves.

"Cape Henry," announced Captain Thompson. "We should reach Jamestown by late afternoon."

Sarah's heart pounded at the news. When she was ten she had held a baby robin in her palm. It was all airy fluff, yet it made her hand tremble with its heartbeat. *Should a giant hold me in its palm at this moment*, thought Sarah, *I'd make its hand tremble with the pounding of my heart, so afraid am I.*

That was not the case with the other passengers. The *Jonathan* had probably never seen such excitement. People began washing their faces, winding their hair, brushing their clothes. Some brought out fresh clothing they had saved especially for their arrival in Jamestown. Each girl looked like a stranger with her fresh-scrubbed face and her clean gown. Anne, Sarah thought, looked very pretty in her green dimity skirt and bodice. Even Rose was scrubbed and dressed, and looking, Sarah decided, quite respectable.

Since she was in mourning and not looking for a husband, Sarah changed into her plain, blue fustian gown. Then, while the others fussed, she stood at the rail and stared at the new world around her.

Her first sight of Virginia was of the white hills of sand and the few pine and fir trees along the shore of Cape Henry. *It's just as barren as I imagined,* Sarah thought. *A hateful place.*

Then they sailed up the James River past the cape and past Point Comfort, and the countryside changed. There were hills around them now, the trees thickened, and the soil looked richer. Some trees and shrubs were in flower. The sight made Sarah long for England. She could almost smell the roses blooming by the front gate and feel the mist of a damp London day upon her face.

Before the summer is over I will smell those roses and feel that mist again, she promised herself, silently acknowledging for the first time her unspoken plan.

Streams and rivers, some surrounded by marshes, now entered the James on both sides. Though there was a gentle breeze, the day felt hot, quite unlike a spring day in England. Even so, the smell of flowers and good, solid earth was sweet.

At the sight of the land, her mother's voice echoed in Sarah's head. "Land," the voice said. "Land is everything."

Sarah's mother had come from a noble family that owned a large estate. The family had prospered until the cost of goods began to rise and rise again. By 1599 Sarah's grandfather had become a penniless nobleman, forced to sell his land to the wealthy merchant from whom he bought his goods. Perhaps that was why her mother had filled Sarah's head with dreams of the land. In England, land meant wealth.

Anne appeared beside Sarah, eager for the new sights. "Look." She pointed to where Richard Kean stood. "It

19

seems the lieutenant has also been busy with his grooming. Even you must admit, Sarah, that he looks very pleasing in blue silk.''

Sarah groaned good-naturedly. ''I agree.

''A settlement,'' she said then, pointing toward a few buildings on the right-hand side of the river. ''Your lieutenant seems to be taking great interest in it.''

''Perhaps it's Martin's Hundred, the plantation he's going to,'' said Anne, shading her eyes to study the place.

When Sarah looked again, Richard had disappeared from the railing.

''Probably he's drunk with the marvel of the New World and has gone to his cabin,'' said a disappointed Anne.

Richard hadn't gone to his cabin. He had circled the deck, and moments later, came up behind them.

''And what do you think of what you see?'' he asked.

Sarah hunched her shoulders and kept her gaze on the shore, but Anne answered eagerly. ''It looks rather beautiful, but untamed. In the midst of the forest I would feel very alone.''

''I hope you'll never have that feeling.'' Richard shuffled his feet, then continued. ''Have I permission to speak to you of a matter close to my heart?''

From the corner of her eye, Sarah saw Anne's eyes widen and her face flush, saw her nod consent. Sarah *felt*, rather than saw, the pointed look Richard gave her, a look that told her to disappear. ''I'll ... ah ... I'll be wanting to see the other shore,'' she muttered, walking away. But she scurried around the quarterdeck and tiptoed back near Anne and Richard, wondering if it were a sin to eavesdrop from behind a barrel.

''You've been in my thoughts,'' Richard told Anne, his back to Sarah. ''Are you, like many other maids aboard, hoping to wed in Virginia?''

"I am." Anne was facing Sarah, and Sarah saw a spark of hope leap into her eyes.

"I, too, am alone," Richard said. "At least I'm alone in Virginia, since my family remains in England."

The light in Anne's eyes dimmed. "Will your wife and young ones be coming to Virginia to join you?" she asked quietly.

"When I spoke of my family I meant my father, Sir William, my mother, Lady Eliza, my brothers and my sisters," he replied. "I'm not married—and I'm not young. I've seen one and thirty years. It's time I took a wife."

Thirty-one years, thought Sarah. Anne was fourteen years younger than he. Goodness, Richard was practically ancient—nearly old enough to be Anne's father. But not too old to be her husband, Sarah told herself quickly.

The sparkle had returned to Anne's eyes, but she had no chance to comment on Richard's words.

"I've been watching you the past few weeks, Mistress Bell," Richard went on. "Your spirits seem as bright as your hair, in spite of all the trials we've encountered on this voyage. Although our stations in life are much different, I could see fit to marry someone such as you. It's not wise for the better classes of people to send their daughters to this harsh new world. At least not until it's more civilized. So, if we wish to wed, it seems some of us gentry must marry persons of lesser quality, persons who can survive the rigors of life in a new land. In short, mistress, I'm asking you to be my wife."

Sarah gasped, nearly giving herself away. Her friend would be the first on board to wed after all, and to Lieutenant Kean, just as Anne had dreamed.

Anne herself appeared stunned; her gaze seemed fixed on the woven gold points tying Richard's right sleeve to his doublet. Long seconds passed before her eyes focused, an icy glint in their depths. She smiled, but it was the first time Sarah had seen no warmth in Anne's smile.

"It was foolish of you to call me a person of lesser quality," she told Richard, her teeth gritted, "for I won't marry a man who sees the union as a favor to me, but a step downward for himself. And don't think you've honored me by your proposal, because I'd rather be the head of the peasants than the tail of the gentry."

Richard's head snapped backward ever so slightly. "The maid has sharp teeth," he commented.

Sarah covered her face, hoping Richard wouldn't strike Anne for insulting him. After all, most English people believed as he did, that some people were superior to others.

When she heard no smack, Sarah dared to peek again.

Anne shrugged. "Forgive me for speaking so plainly. Perhaps there's another woman on board who would suit you, since you are willing to marry below your station," she said, barely managing to keep the sarcasm from her voice. "Perhaps Mistress Rose Hawkings. I'm sure she would make a man a willing wife."

Sarah choked back a laugh.

Richard chose to ignore Anne's sly mockery and simply shook his head. "Most others of marrying age are either bubbleheaded wenches or sickly. My job—protecting English lives from murdering savages—will be difficult. Of course, my mere military presence will no doubt frighten the natives so much, we'll be able to live in peace in Martin's Hundred." He heaved a sigh. "Yet I hope for a wife to share my burden and my days."

His forlorn tone as he said the last words must have softened Anne's heart, for when she answered, her voice was more gentle. "Forgive me," she told him. "It won't be me." And there it ended.

The sun was setting behind the hills as Richard tramped away. Sarah scurried out from behind the barrel. "I heard it all," she whispered.

"No doubt you think I'm crazy for refusing him."

Sarah shook her head. "He has lost much more than you have. You would have taught him to laugh and be jolly. Do you realize we've never seen him smile?"

"You're right," Anne agreed. She paused. "I wonder if he has all his teeth?"

Their hoots of laughter were halted by a shout that was soon echoed around the *Jonathan* in excited whispers. "Jamestown!"

Chapter 4

Sarah and Anne leaned over the starboard rail, watching silently as the ship sailed nearer the settlement. "Just think, Sarah," Anne said, "tonight we'll sleep on something that isn't rolling beneath us. I can hardly wait."

But Anne was to be disappointed, for after the *Jonathan* was tethered to trees on the bank, Captain Thompson announced it was too late to go ashore.

Groans rose into the darkening sky. "One more night on this wretched ship," sighed Anne.

"Yes, one more night," Sarah answered, secretly relieved. Although the *Jonathan* was squalid, and Sarah would have loved to be back on land after seven weeks at sea, she felt safe on the ship. Besides, the only land she wanted to be on was England. She was happy to spend another night on board if it delayed her setting foot in Virginia.

How could anyone look forward to living in Jamestown? Sarah wondered, staring at the settlement. "I think it's a miserable-looking place," she confessed to Anne. "And smelly, too, the captain said. There's a swamp nearby that stinks when the weather's hot. I'm glad I can't smell it now."

Anne ignored Sarah's comments and continued to study their new home. The fort itself squatted on a low, flat neck of land jutting into the river. By May 1620, the town had outgrown the original triangular palisade with its half-moon bastions protecting each corner. Houses now spilled outside its walls.

"Look," said Anne. "The palisade is made from tree trunks sunk upright into the ground. What a lot of work that must have been."

"More work than the houses were." Sarah stared at the plain, thatched-roof houses. Their walls, made from tree branches, were plastered with clay and straw.

"There's nothing the matter with wattle-and-daub houses," said Anne. "Many English folk still live in them."

"Look, there are a few houses made of wooden timbers." Sarah pointed inside the palisade. *I'll take them over wattle and daub, thank you,* she thought, watching the increasing bustle on shore and on the water as news of their arrival spread. She wondered if Aunt Mary's Charles were among those scurrying about in the fading light or rowing madly toward the town from the outlying settlements.

"The sky looks as though a giant tossed a handful of glistening sugar heavenward," murmured Anne a while later. She had convinced Sarah to spend the night on deck. The girls were sitting on their pallets, their backs against a nearby crate. "And listen to how quiet the ship is now that we're at anchor. No loud creaking and groaning."

Sarah's thoughts were not on the Virginia sky nor on the silence of the ship. "Aren't you afraid?" she said to Anne. "I've heard such dreadful stories of Virginia. Stories of starving and disease, of the savages."

Anne flapped a hand at Sarah. "We survived the voyage with its putrid food and water, its fever. It won't be nearly as bad here in Virginia."

"But what about the Indians? The thought of an Indian makes me shiver."

"Pish! Didn't you see the Indian Pocahontas when she was in London in 1616?"

Sarah shook her head. "I heard about her, though."

"I saw her one day, riding through the streets with her Indian companions. Yes, they have dusky skin, but I think they're a handsome people. Don't worry, Sarah, we have nothing to fear from the natives of Virginia."

"I pray you're right," Sarah said, twisting a piece of her hair around and around a finger. "But I can't help wondering what Father would have thought of the land Aunt Mary's dreams have brought me to." Her voice cracked, and she covered her face with her hands. "Oh, Anne, why did Aunt Mary bring me here? And why did she have to die, like everyone I've ever loved? I miss her so much, but I'm so angry at her I could bellow like a mad bull."

"So, bellow." Anne put her arm around Sarah and gave her a squeeze.

Instead of bellowing, Sarah wept. For her mother, for her father, for Aunt Mary, for herself. When her tears dried, the girls lay down to snatch a few hours of sleep.

A noisy swarm of people on shore woke Sarah and Anne the next morning.

Anne gasped. "There must be nearly four hundred," she said, gaping at the men dressed in leather doublets and breeches, some with cocky plumes in their cavalier hats. The rising sun glittered off the swords and fowling-pieces carried by a few. Stunned by the sight, the women on board fell silent.

Quickly Anne scrubbed at her face with a corner of

her hem and smoothed her hair. "Do I look all right?" she asked, a crease between her brows.

Soon the gangplank was lowered, and the passengers were leaving the *Jonathan*. Sarah held back, letting the "brides" go ahead. "Go on," she told Anne. "Don't wait for me."

"I'll wait," Anne said, then added, "Oh, Sarah, suddenly my heart is pounding like the heart of a caged rabbit, and my courage has fled. I'm not sure I'm brave enough to go ashore and face that mob of men."

"Then you better find your courage again," said Sarah, her head bobbing, "because if you don't go, no one will ever get me off this ship."

Anne's back straightened. "Come on," she said, her voice sure once again.

"Have you seen your aunt's fiancé, Sarah?" she asked as they joined the crowd inching toward the gangplank.

Sarah had searched the throng for Charles, but hadn't seen his towering frame among the shifting men. Perhaps Falling Creek was too far upriver for him to have arrived yet.

Anne's palm on Sarah's back nudged her gently along the gangplank. She drew back as hands reached out from all sides, offering to help her take her first step on land. That step was a wobbly one, for the earth wasn't steady. It rocked and swayed beneath her feet. Without thinking, she grabbed the nearest arm to steady herself.

"Henry's got hisself a good 'un," someone yelled, and Sarah looked at her rescuer. She couldn't tell how old he was, but he had a face like a dried plum and as many teeth as a plum has pits. He grinned at her eagerly, his eyes fairly bursting from his head.

Sarah shrank back. Speaking to a strange man was bad enough, but to be touched by one . . . She looked frantically from man to man, hoping to see the familiar face of Charles in the crowd.

Then Anne slipped an arm through hers. "Don't raise your hopes," she told the dried plum called Henry. "She's not one of the marrying maids and is not looking for a husband." She smiled at the man. "My friend thanks you for your help," she said, giving Sarah a jab with her elbow, "but I'm sure she has her land legs again."

Sarah managed a silent, open-mouthed nod.

"Too bad, Henry. That 'un got away," someone called.

"No matter," another voice remarked. "Henry doesn't have permission to marry anyway."

Henry gave Sarah a cheerful wink and turned to the next woman in line, as Anne and Sarah took their first steps on Virginia soil.

Chapter 5

"Your bath's all ready," said Mistress Pierce a while later, pouring a final cauldron of steaming water into the wooden tub squatting beside the fireplace. "The captain's off on business and won't be home till later, so no need to worry about being interrupted."

Since there was no guesthouse in Jamestown, Anne and Sarah had been placed in the home of Captain William Pierce and his wife, where they would stay until permanent arrangements were made.

"You go first," Anne told Sarah.

As she started to undress, Sarah looked around at the Pierces' house. She had been pleased to see it was one of the few two-storied, timbered houses she had noticed earlier. There were two rooms on the ground floor—the main room containing the fireplace, and the Pierces' bedroom. Stairs led up to another room, where the girls would sleep.

As she slipped out of her undergarments, Sarah noticed that the house seemed about to collapse. Daylight showed between some rotten-looking timbers, and the roof beams sagged. "Perhaps a wattle-and-daub house would be better," she whispered to Anne, darting a few pointed glances toward the nearest decaying wood.

Anne gave Sarah a sharp look as Mistress Pierce, a warm-hearted soul who must have seen Sarah's glance, said, "It's the climate. Wood just doesn't hold up for long. Now, tell me, what did you think of the governor's speech?"

Governor Yeardley, his wife, and members of the Council had been waiting to greet the passengers of the *Jonathan*.

"The governor gave a most rousing speech of welcome," Anne told Mistress Pierce. "And the sight of the gold braid and the silk and satin almost made me forget London is an ocean away."

It didn't make me forget, thought Sarah. In fact, she'd deemed the elegant clothing rather absurd, considering the surroundings. She hadn't seen a single cobbled street in Jamestown, and the only vehicles she'd seen were a couple of two-wheeled carts outside the palisade and some low sledges dragged by oxen in a nearby field. Mostly what she'd seen was tobacco. It seemed the colonists had gone tobacco crazy. It was planted everywhere, even in the streets.

"They look as though they're about to visit the court of James," Sarah had told Anne with a giggle, after the governor's speech, "yet they live in a town where the streets are dirt paths planted with sotweed, and there isn't a single horse or carriage in sight. Don't you think it silly?"

All she'd gotten for her humor was a hard look from Anne. And now, after her remark about the decaying house, she'd gotten another. With a sigh, half regret, half relief, Sarah slipped into the bathwater, where she stayed until her skin wrinkled like a walnut shell, getting out only when Mistress Pierce good-naturedly threatened to make her haul more water for Anne if she didn't vacate the tub at once.

When Captain Pierce arrived a couple of hours later,

Sarah gathered enough courage to speak to the man and asked him to find out where Charles was. "He came to Virginia last year with a team of men under Captain Bluett," she mumbled into her shoes. "They were to build an ironworks at a place called Falling Creek. Aunt Mary had one letter from him, mailed just after he got here."

"Perhaps you missed him in the crowd," Mistress Pierce suggested.

Sarah doubted she had, since Charles was an enormous man, nearly impossible to miss in a crowd of any size. He was so large that whenever Sarah thought of Charles Littlefield, she thought of oxen. Charles, an ironworker with great brawny shoulders, shaggy black hair, and huge, gnarled hands, had the look and strength of an ox. But he also had the ox's gentle eye and manner, and its patience.

"He's probably on his way," Captain Pierce said.

Mistress Pierce pursed her lips. "Oh dear. I don't think it's a good idea for an unmarried man to be responsible for a young girl," she said.

Sarah took a breath. The time had come to share her plan. She only hoped Anne wouldn't be too disappointed in her. "Charles's only duty will be to pay my fare back to England," she said quietly. "I plan to return as soon as possible, on the *Jonathan*, if I can."

Anne gasped. "Oh, Sarah, no! There's nothing to go back for, no one waiting to welcome you home. Please stay and give Virginia a chance."

"Virginia needs young women," Captain Pierce said gruffly. "Even ones who mumble so, these old ears can't hear them," he added under his breath.

"You and your aunt paid your fares to sail to Virginia?" Mistress Pierce asked.

Sarah nodded.

"Then you simply can't go," the older woman said, her white hair bobbing. "You'd lose your headright."

Sarah had heard about headrights during the voyage. Anyone who paid his or her own fare or another person's fare to come to the colony before 1625 got fifty acres of land. Sarah was entitled to one hundred acres, fifty for herself, fifty for her aunt.

But land would tie her to Virginia, and she wanted nothing to hold her here, not even the chance to fulfill her mother's dream of owning land. She shook her head, and no amount of persuasion or argument would change her mind.

"Ah, well," said Captain Pierce, and went off to ask about Charles.

An hour later he was back, the spiky tufts of his beetle brows drawn downward. Sarah caught her breath as the captain took her hand between his huge ones, but something in his eyes kept her from jerking it away. "I'm sorry, my dear," he said, leading Sarah to a stool. "Charles Littlefield is dead."

Mistress Pierce scurried for a noggin of ale, then held it to Sarah's lips.

"Poor dear," Mistress Pierce clucked. "First her aunt, now Master Littlefield."

Sarah waited, expecting a flood of grief to drown her. Though he wasn't related, Charles was the closest thing to family she'd had left in the world. Surprised when the sorrow didn't come, Sarah pushed herself to her feet, took a shuddering breath, and said, "Please . . . tell me what . . . happened."

"According to Company records, Master Littlefield took a fever soon after he arrived in Jamestown. He never did reach Falling Creek, for he died within a month."

"That's very common, you know," interrupted his wife. "Many people sicken right off. No doubt some of the maids who sailed with you already lie shaking with flux or fever. Poor dears. They arrive with dreams of a wedding, and soon it's doubtful they'll live to choose a husband.'' She clucked her tongue and was quiet, then crooked her neck to peer into Sarah's face, as though checking to see if the tears had come.

''No-o-o-o-o-o!'' Sarah's cry was one of anger, not sorrow.

Mistress Pierce jumped back. Anne clutched Sarah's hand, looking startled and bewildered at the same time.

''He was dead all this time,'' Sarah hissed. ''Dead before we left England. Had we known, we would have stayed, and Aunt Mary would still be alive!''

Anne covered her mouth with her hands, and tears rimmed her eyes. The Pierces simply shook their heads.

Sarah thought back to Aunt Mary's death in the stinking hold, her hand reaching toward the light she hadn't seen in days. And strangely enough, that memory sent the anger out of her. She plopped onto the stool again, waving Anne away when she bent to comfort her. She took another sip of Mistress Pierce's ale.

''Remember, Anne?'' she asked then. ''Remember Aunt Mary's words, just before she died? She said, 'Charles. Waiting.' ''

Anne nodded, but her frown told Sarah she didn't understand. ''Don't you see?'' Sarah insisted. ''Aunt Mary has her Charles after all.''

Chapter 6

"So what are you going to do?" Anne asked a short while later.

Sarah shook her head. "I don't know. With Charles dead, I have no one to pay my fare home."

"I doubt Master Littlefield would have had enough money to pay your passage anyway," said Mistress Pierce, overhearing. "Money's scarce in Virginia. Mostly we trade for what we need. And what we trade is tobacco. Anne's new husband will even pay her fare in tobacco. One hundred and twenty pounds to be exact."

"Humph!" snorted Anne. "I'm worth less than my weight in tobacco? I certainly hope the price per pound is high."

"No matter how high, whoever marries you will be getting a bargain," Sarah told her. Then she sighed. "So, since I have no money and nothing worth trading, what I need is tobacco. But how do I get it? Pluck it from the plants growing in the streets?"

Mistress Pierce chuckled. "You don't seem the type to steal another person's leaves. Besides, it's cured tobacco they'll be wanting, not green. You'll have to earn it—or grow it yourself."

"She can't grow it herself now, can she?" snapped Anne, "since she has no land—and doesn't want any," she added pointedly. "So she'll have to earn it."

"You might indenture yourself," said Captain Pierce, who was sitting on a stool smoking his pipe.

Sarah gasped. "You mean be someone's servant?"

"Our indentured servants are valuable members of the colony," said Captain Pierce with a frown. "For many, it's the only way they can get ahead in the world. You can be sure if a person is willing to indenture himself, he desires to better himself as well. And in doing so, he betters Virginia."

Chastened, Sarah looked at the floor.

"It must be a hard life," said Anne.

Captain Pierce tugged at his beard. "Not always. Indentures last from four to seven years, more for a child. Skilled workers practice their trade. Children must be taught their letters and their numbers, and sometimes a trade as well. Have you a trade?" he asked Sarah abruptly, peering at her with narrowed eyes.

"She can sew," Anne answered quickly.

"A straight seam only," Sarah explained, not looking directly at the captain. "I can't cut or fit. When I return to England I plan to apprentice myself to a seamstress."

"You won't be returning to England, dear, unless you earn your passage," Mistress Pierce reminded her. "But indenturing yourself isn't the answer anyway. Servants get only their upkeep, sometimes freedom dues— money or land when they earn their freedom."

"So, if I do indenture myself, it will be at least four years before I can return home," said Sarah with a groan, "and then only if I receive some freedom dues."

"As a servant, she wouldn't be allowed to marry without permission either," Captain Pierce added.

Mistress Pierce clapped her hands to her head. "Marry! That's it! Why don't you join the other maids and find a husband? Then you won't have to worry about fares or indentures."

Sarah gave the Pierces a look of panic. "I'm only fourteen," she told them. "I'm not ready to marry."

"Fourteen's old enough to my way of thinking," snorted Mistress Pierce.

Anne slipped an arm over Sarah's shoulders. "Sarah has had a very sheltered life," she explained. "Her father and Master Littlefield were practically the only men she has ever known."

Mistress Pierce's eyebrows rose. "I'm certain that situation will change quickly here in Virginia," she said, "with so many men and so few women. But you're not obliged to marry unless you want to." She smacked her hands together. "Now, enough talk. The governor and his wife have invited all newcomers to tea. After that, the courting begins. Sarah's problem will simply have to wait until later. Come, we'll show you the way."

"My future seems to hold few choices," Sarah groaned to Anne, as they followed the Pierces toward the Governor's Mansion.

"Aye," agreed Anne. "Either you become a servant or you become a wife."

"Neither of those choices will get me home to England. Perhaps I shouldn't refuse my headright. But, oh, Anne, what would I do with land?" She flicked a finger at a tobacco plant, then at a tree. "I haven't the vaguest idea how to grow tobacco, but I do know the monstrous trees would have to be cleared before I could even begin to plant. And how could I build a house?" She sighed. "No, claiming my headright is not the answer."

Mistress Pierce dropped back to walk beside them. "The Yeardleys are a charming couple," she chattered, as they neared the crowd surrounding the Governor's

Mansion. "She came here as a child in 1609, you know."

She waved at a man standing near the governor. "That's John Rolfe, our son-in-law. After his poor Indian princess Pocahontas died in England, he married our daughter. He's the man who developed the strain of tobacco plant that flourishes here," she added, her voice full of pride.

Captain Pierce pointed out a round, little man who was busy sampling the beer. "John Pory," he explained. "He's the secretary for the Council, the one you go to if you change your mind and apply for your headright." From the table beside Master Pory the captain chose a full wooden noggin for each of them.

"What is this?" Anne asked, when she had taken a sip from hers.

"Oh, we can make liquor to sweeten our lips,
Of pumpkins, of parsnips, of walnut-tree chips,"

quoted Mistress Pierce with a laugh, "but this is beer made from a native fruit we call the Indian plum or persimmon."

"It's very strange, but delicious," Anne said, taking a bigger sip.

"Be careful you don't drink too much," warned Sarah, "or you might choose the wrong husband in the courting." She edged nearer her friend. "Already many eyes are looking your way," she whispered, peeking sideways at the curious and eager faces around them, and preferring to think they were ogling Anne, but not her.

When the tea ended, the courting began. The maids were led to the green with the eligible men hustling after.

"Such a hotchpotch of people I never did see!" exclaimed Mistress Pierce. "How can any woman tell the knaves from the decent, respectable men with all this dithering and confusion?"

Sarah gave Anne a hug. "Be careful making your choice," she said, before going to stand by the Pierces and watch as Anne, with a hesitant smile, but a determined stride, entered the matchmaking.

Chapter 7

Anne was immediately surrounded by several men, and Sarah lost sight of her. Then she saw Richard Kean among the onlookers, his eyes fixed on the spot where Anne had disappeared into the mob. His mouth drew downward in stark contrast to his upwardly curving mustache; his shoulders slumped in a most unmilitary fashion.

Why, he's sorry Anne rejected him, Sarah thought. *Perhaps he has a heart after all.*

The crowd drifted into clusters, each maid encircled by men seeking to woo her. Rejected suitors scurried among the clusters, searching for an overlooked maid. Simply watching made Sarah feel faint. *How horrible,* she thought, *to be enclosed by all those strange, desperate men.* Shuddering, Sarah was about to return to the Pierces, where she could think about her future in peace, when a man leaped to her side.

"Me name's Dave Dixon and I've fifty acres up Weyanoke way. I've seen five and thirty years, had me one wife, who died, have no wee 'uns, don't spit on the floor—much, and scrub meself at least once a month. Will ya marry me?"

Sarah's eyes flew wide and her tongue stuck to the

roof of her mouth. She was about to laugh, or scream, she wasn't certain which, when Mistress Pierce stepped to her side.

"Go on with you now, Dave Dixon," she told the man, whose eyes were looking at Sarah the way a child looks at a sweet. "Pin your hopes on another lass. This one isn't in the runnin'." And she gave the man a gentle push on his leather-clad shoulder.

Sarah gave the woman a grateful smile over her shoulder and fled as though hellhounds were at her heels. Her heart was still thudding when she passed a grove of trees so thick it looked like a bulky wall rising from the earth. Something about the grove felt familiar, so she slowed and peered into its black shadows.

Then Sarah remembered waking the night before to find her cheeks wet with tears. She had been dreaming of standing next to a forest, peering into its depths, just as she now tried to peer into the grove. She had entered the dream forest and had seen the face of her mother floating through the trees in a veil of mist. "Sa-a-ar-rah," she called.

Sarah had run toward her mother, only to have her face fade and reappear in another spot. Then her father's face appeared, then Aunt Mary's, then her mother's again. Once even Charles drifted through the leaves calling her name. "Sarah," they droned in hollow voices. "Sa-a-ar-a-ah."

Frantically, Sarah had run from one face to another, only to have each melt away when she came near. She had awakened sobbing, her heart clutched with grief and loneliness.

Now, as she stood peering into the forest of Virginia, the same feelings overwhelmed her. Sarah sank down, buried her head in her hands, and wept. For the first time she felt in her heart, in her soul, what it meant to be truly alone in the world.

Sarah thought of Anne, who at that moment was choosing a mate to share her life with, and wept anew. She had allowed Anne to become too dear to her, and now she was losing her, too.

At last, exhausted by her tears and a bit calmer, Sarah drew back her shoulders and went on her way. She had scarcely any quiet time to think about her future though, for soon after, Mistress Pierce returned home. An hour later Anne appeared, breathless, her cheeks nearly as red as her hair.

"Oh, Sarah," Anne said with a laugh, "never have I been so fawned over. Why, the difficult part will not be finding a good man, it will be making a choice from all those who made me an offer. There is an Isaac and a Henry, a Richard, a Matthew, and a Samuel. Goodness, I can scarce remember the faces that go with the names!"

"Watch out for the Henry," Sarah warned her. "If he's the one who greeted us when we landed, he must be indentured, because he's not able to marry. I think he merely enjoys the quest."

"Don't worry, it's not that wizened-face one," said Anne, "and I've told all my suitors I must think over their offers before I decide. But there's one who makes my heart trip a little faster, yet, strangely enough, also brings me comfort." She brushed a few damp straggles of wavy, red hair off her forehead.

"His name is Cisly Mills," she continued. "He has his own house in Martin's Hundred, ten miles down-river. And once he pays my fare, he can claim my headright and will have one hundred of acres of land—just like you," she added, her finger stabbing the air between them. "Imagine, Sarah, one hundred acres of land all your own. Only the wealthy yeomen and the landed gentry in England have that much land." Anne closed her eyes, tilted her head back, crossed her arms, and hugged herself. "Never did I dream I might some-day be mistress of a great estate!"

Sarah smiled stiffly and nodded. When she thought of the land she could claim, a vision of a giant anchor embedded in the earth flashed into her mind. A rope was tied to the anchor and the other end was wrapped around her neck. A burden tying her to Virginia. That's what land meant to Sarah.

"And you should have seen Rose," Anne continued, laughter nearly choking her. "She tried so hard to appear respectable, but I fear Shakespeare would not have wanted her in his plays, for she is not a good actor. And what do you suppose she went and did?" Anne clapped her hands and prattled on, without giving Sarah a chance to guess. "Why, she's promised herself to two different men, saying she'll decide later which one will be honored with her acceptance. Of course, she didn't tell the two men she already promised another. Woe to Rose should they discover both are to wed the same woman!"

Anne began to giggle, and since her bell-like laughter made anyone hearing her feel happier, Sarah's black mood lifted a bit. Woe indeed! It would be interesting to learn the result of Rose's wiles. Sarah doubted they would have to wait long, for most weddings were to take place as soon as possible, so the men could return to their settlements. Already the Reverends Buck, Mease, and Bargrave were hearing vows and giving blessings.

A short time later, as Sarah and Anne were helping Mistress Pierce with the evening meal, they heard distant shouts and thunderous oaths. Sarah's stomach fluttered with fear. "Indians?" she asked.

Mistress Pierce shook her head. "Probably some young hotheads who can't keep the peace for a single day," she grumbled. "Go on. See what the skirmish is about."

As the girls were leaving, a young man came dashing to the door. "Mistress Bell," he said. "I'm glad I found you. I was hoping to escort you to the scene of the quarrel. The reason for it will bring a smile to your rosy lips, I'll wager."

"Why, Cisly Mills, whatever do you mean?" Anne asked.

Sarah realized the young man was the one who had Anne in such turmoil. They did make a perfect couple. His hair was even redder than Anne's, and across his nose and cheeks splotches of freckles marched in disarray. His eyes were the color of the sky on a rainy day, yet sparkled with good humor.

"Why, it's Jacob Howe and Hugh Leaven," he stated, as though that explained everything. When Anne looked puzzled, he added, "You know, the two men that dark-haired wench promised to marry."

"Rose!" exclaimed Anne. Sarah grinned.

"The dolts at last discovered what the rest of us already knew," laughed Cisly. "The two are by the shore preparing to fight it out. If I had a tuppence to wager, I do believe I'd put my money on Hugh Leaven."

When they reached the edge of the crowd surrounding the two men, Sarah decided Cisly's tuppence would have been safe enough. If there were going to be a fight, Hugh Leaven would surely be the victor. He was immensely tall and strong with a chest like a water cask.

Sarah wondered why Rose had even looked at Jacob Howe. He was a narrow, stringy man with tufts of pale hair sticking out in all directions, as though undecided which way they should lie.

At that moment Governor Yeardley came puffing up,

frantically tucking his shirt into his breeches. Behind him came Captain Pierce with Rose.

The governor thrust Rose into the center of the circle where the two men stood. "Now, girl," he said, "we'll have this matter settled. Make your choice."

The onlookers gave a massive sigh of disappointment at being done out of their fight. Hugh Leaven grinned, gap-toothed, at the governor's statement, certain Rose would choose him. Jacob Howe tried to look as though he didn't care that Rose was sure to pick Hugh.

Sarah nudged Anne. "Hugh looks well-suited to Rose. Likely she'll pick him. What do you think?"

Anne nodded, but Sarah noticed she was looking not at Rose and her suitors, but only at Cisly.

Rose stood, her hands upon her hips, her elbows akimbo, her chin against her bosom. She peered at the two men from under her lowered eyebrows, looking first at one, then the other. At last she raised an arm and pointed a long, bony finger.

"You," she said, and pointed at Jacob Howe.

The crowd gasped. Hugh Leaven shook his gnarled fist in Jacob's direction and tramped out of the circle. Jacob tugged at a tuft of his hair and grinned foolishly.

"So be it," muttered Governor Yeardley. "Jacob Howe you shall wed." Turning to Master Sharpless, the pimple-pocked clerk of the General Assembly, who stood nearby, he said, "Send for the Reverend Buck."

"No need," said the minister, stepping through the crowd.

There and then Rose and Jacob Howe were wed. When the vows were said, Jacob leaned forward as though to kiss her, but Rose waved him away. "Hands off," she told him. "You'll not be kissin' me lessen I give you leave."

Jacob hesitated, tugged again at a tuft of hair. Then suddenly he grabbed Rose behind the neck with one

44

hand, threw his other arm around her, pulled her to him and kissed her soundly. A cheer went up.

"Now come," he ordered. "Fetch your belongings. If we're to be home before sunrise, you best move your scrawny carcass." Off he stalked, a bewildered Rose trailing after.

Chapter 8

After Rose and her new husband had disappeared, Sarah, Anne, and Cisly started back to the Pierces' through the late-afternoon sunlight, Anne and Cisly dawdling behind.

As she walked, Sarah worried about her future. How could she earn her fare back to England? What was to become of her? Was there no way she could survive in this world other than being a servant or a wife?

Servant or wife. Servant or wife. The words went around and around in her head.

A handful of children tumbled across the path playing squat-tag. Seeing them brought Captain Pierce's words to mind: "Children must be taught their letters and their numbers." Suddenly Sarah knew how she could earn her fare. She slowed her steps, not thinking that she might be interrupting a private moment between Anne and Cisly.

"Master Mills," she said hesitantly, lowering her head. "Are there any indentured children in Martin's Hundred?"

"Please call me Cisly," he said, and the friendliness in his voice made Sarah feel more at ease with him.

"And yes, there are indentured children in Martin's Hundred. A few."

"Is anyone teaching them their . . . their letters and numbers?"

Cisly scratched his head. "I don't believe so. Most folks have little time for their own work."

"Then Martin's Hundred needs a tutor. Do you know whom I might . . . might speak with about such a position?"

"The burgesses from our hundred are in town," Cisly said, naming the two men from Martin's Hundred who had been elected to the council in Jamestown. "They've come to greet the new chief lieutenant who arrived on the *Jonathan* with you. I suppose they'd be the ones to see."

Sarah chewed a fingernail thoughtfully for a moment, then clasped her hands together, gathered her courage, and asked, "Could you take me to them?"

"Oh, Sarah," whispered Anne, as Cisly led them toward the river. "What a wonderful idea. We could be together in Martin's Hundred. You don't know what it would mean to me to have a friend by my side."

"Then you've given Cisly your word?"

Anne shook her head. "He hasn't asked proper yet. But I'm certain he will."

By now they were nearing the shore, and Sarah saw four men clustered near a shallop, a large, one-masted, open-deck boat. A few steps more and she saw Richard Kean was one of them. Cisly approached the men, but Anne's steps faltered. "I'll wait here," she said.

Sarah clutched at Anne's arm, realizing her friend did not want to encounter Richard when she was with Cisly. "Please, Anne, stay by me. You give me courage."

Anne sighed. "Very well."

Cisly beckoned to Sarah and Anne. "This is Master

47

Jackson and Master Boys," he said. "You know Lieutenant Kean." The three men bowed, although Richard's eyes never left Anne's face as he did so.

Master Boys turned to the fourth man, standing apart from the rest. "This is John Clark," he said. The man nodded, his smile crinkling his eyes and highlighting the scar on his right cheek, a mirror image of the one Richard had under his left eye.

Sarah noticed the dark look Richard shot Master Boys and John Clark. She had no time to wonder about it, for Cisly said, "Mistress Douglas is seeking information about Martin's Hundred."

Sarah opened her mouth, but no words came out. Anne gave her a jab in the back, before saying, "We learned there are some indentured children in Martin's Hundred who must be schooled. Sarah is wondering if you need a tutor. She's well-suited for the job." She gave Sarah another jab.

At last Sarah found her voice, though thin and crackly it was. "I . . . I am well-learned," she stuttered, looking at no one in particular. "My father was a schoolteacher and spent all his free time tutoring me."

Master Jackson shook his head. "We have only a handful of children, not enough to warrant a full-time tutor."

Anne let out a sigh, and Sarah's shoulders drooped.

"But if you're willing to spend only part of your day teaching reluctant young minds and part of your day in other tasks," said Master Jackson, "I'm certain Martin's Hundred would welcome you. We need all sorts of willing workers for our settlement."

Anne clapped her hands in glee, causing the three strangers to grin at her. Even Richard allowed a tiny twitch to tug at the corners of his mouth.

"I cannot believe it!" said Anne. "We'll be together in . . ." She stopped and slapped a hand over her mouth, as though suddenly remembering Cisly hadn't asked her to marry him, and unless he did, Sarah would be going to Martin's Hundred without her.

Cisly chuckled. Then to Sarah's amazement, he knelt in the mud at the shore and took Anne's hand in his. "Mistress Bell," he said, "will you do me the honor of becoming my wife?"

Sarah couldn't tell if Anne's face turned as red as her hair because of a blush or because the setting sun was pointing crimson fingers across the heavens toward them. Anne covered her face with her free palm and took a deep breath, before dropping her hand and saying, "Only if these good gentlemen will attest to your character and to the fine home and land you boast of."

The burgesses from Martin's Hundred burst into laughter. Then Master Boys said, "A finer citizen of the New World you couldn't find anywhere. Cisly is indeed of upstanding character, and he does have a snug house and a claim to fifty acres of rich Virginia soil."

"Now he can claim fifty more," said Anne with a smile, which was her way of saying yes. Cisly sent a whoop into the sky, while Sarah hugged her friend and wished her well.

Richard Kean seemed to find no joy in the moment. His look was as dark as the one he had given John Clark earlier, as dark as the forest surrounding Jamestown, a forest that seemed to creep in on the settlement, Sarah thought, as the day grew older. An animal howled in the distance. A wolf, Sarah decided, and shivered.

"Meet us here tomorrow," Master Jackson said. "We sail downriver at noon."

"Is there some reason Lieutenant Kean would be angry at John Clark?" Sarah asked Cisly, as they walked home. "Richard gave him a wrathful look when Master Boys introduced John."

"He gave Master Boys a terrible look too," said Anne.

"Perhaps he thought John didn't deserve to be introduced, since he's indentured," Cisly said.

"That would explain it," Anne agreed. "Richard has lofty thoughts about his position in life."

"You'd think he'd be more humble after you refused his proposal of marriage and called him the tail of the gentry," said Sarah with a giggle.

Cisly gave Anne a startled look. *Oh, no,* Sarah thought. *What have I done? First I can't find my voice around a man, and now I blabber too much.*

But Cisly only smiled. "It doesn't surprise me that Richard Kean tried to claim Anne's hand," he said. "I'm only grateful that she refused him." He took Anne's hand in his and raised it to his lips.

Sarah dared to breathe again.

∞∞∞
Chapter 9

A nne and Cisly were married the next morning in a simple ceremony on the green near the Governor's mansion. Then Cisly went off to claim his new land while Anne and Sarah packed. Well before lunch he was back, and it was time to thank the Pierces and say good-bye.

Sarah watched as her two wooden chests were carted off by a couple of sturdy men. The contents of the chests didn't seem like much with which to survive life in a new land. Indeed, when Sarah thought of all they had left behind in England, she felt like weeping. She and Aunt Mary had sold all the household belongings to raise money for their fares and some provisions.

Sarah had managed to stay dry-eyed as the furniture was hauled away, though her heart wrenched when her father's desk disappeared down the lane. She did weep when the man came for her father's books, and though she knew there was room only for belongings that would help them survive in Virginia, she had kept a few. Now, she was glad she had. They would be useful in her new position as tutor.

She followed Anne and Cisly as the chests holding those books were carried to the shore.

They were nearing the palisade gate when Sarah saw a tall, strange-looking man. "An Indian!" she gasped.

"Yes, an Indian," said Anne, "though he isn't dressed in English clothing, as were the Indians I saw in London."

Though Cisly and the chest bearers took no notice of the native as he walked through the gate like any other visitor, both Sarah and Anne stared. Sarah was glad of her long skirts; they hid her knocking knees.

Half the man's head was shaved, while on the other half his hair was long and knotted behind his ear. He was naked except for a fringed apron of animal skin around his middle, three feathers on his head, and strings of beads about his neck and wrists. He carried a bow, and a quiver made from a wolf's hide—with the wolf's head still attached. The quiver was tied around his waist with the tail of another animal, the end of which hung down behind him. From the front, it looked as though the tail grew from the Indian himself.

As he neared them, Sarah saw dark arrows and crosses tattooed into the skin on his shoulders, breast, and legs. "Look," she whispered to Anne, when something green and yellow moved near the Indian's shoulder. "He has a snake dangling from a hole in his ear. O-o-oh, it's alive!"

The girls lifted their skirts and scurried to catch up with Cisly. "He is a fine figure of a man," puffed Anne as they ran. "Only his strange dress and ornament make him seem different from Cisly."

"You can believe that if you wish," said Sarah, as they slowed their pace, "but I doubt I'll ever feel comfortable around a savage."

Masters Jackson and Boys, John Clark, and Richard were at the shore, and soon the girls' chests were wedged among the barrels and crates already on board the roomy deck of the waiting shallop. Sarah sat with

Anne and Cisly on the thwart nearest the bow of the open boat. John shoved off, hoisted the single sail, then seated himself to one side of the sailing thwart. Master Jackson, at the rudder, pointed the boat downriver. Richard stood, one foot on the opposite end of the thwart upon which John sat.

Master Boys plunked himself beside Sarah. She resisted the urge to slide away, but under a fold of her skirt, her hands clenched into a ball.

"Even though the tide is with us, it will be near dusk before we make Martin's Hundred. I trust the journey won't be tiresome for you," said Master Boys.

"Indeed not," said Anne on the other side of Sarah. "There are so many things to look at, most new to our eye and ear. I never saw so many trees in England, so thick and far-reaching. Look, Sarah, how they stand apart yet cast a deep shade. And there's little undergrowth beneath them."

"It's a pity the pigeons haven't flown over today," said Master Boys. "At times the flock is so immense it takes three or four hours to pass, and the noise of their wings is like thunder. They make good eating too." With that he rubbed his lean stomach and turned to a pack beside him, from which he removed the well-browned carcass of a large bird, which he tore into pieces and handed around. "Turkey," he explained when Richard's eyebrows rose at the sight of his portion. "William Spense trapped it yesterday, along with three larger ones."

Sarah didn't know if it was the fresh air or being so long without good food that gave her such an appetite, but suddenly she was starved.

"Why are you not as large as a cow?" Cisly teased from the other side of Anne, when Sarah finally tossed her last turkey bone to the fish. "You eat enough for two men." The others laughed, and Sarah wished she could hide her blushing face in her skirts.

"She's still a growing girl," announced Anne, patting Sarah's knee, before handing her a handkerchief to wipe her fingers.

"Is the James the river the merchant adventurers hoped would lead them to India?" Richard asked then.

Master Jackson nodded. "Aye. What foolish ideas they had when they started the Virginia Company. And what disappointment when they found no passage to India, and no gold lying on the ground for the picking."

Richard twisted one end of his mustache into a tidier curl. "At least the Spanish have been denied the land," he said, his tone implying he had personally kept the Spaniards from putting a toe on Virginia soil.

He seemed about to say more when a fish came sailing over the side of the boat and began flopping about at their feet. It was nearly four feet long and covered with bony plates. Under its long, ugly snout were thick, sucking lips, near which some fleshy finger-like whiskers protruded.

"Ah-h-h," Sarah squealed, scrambling onto the wooden seat, where Anne soon joined her.

Quickly John Clark clouted the animal on the head with an ax handle he'd been carving.

Richard stepped forward, flicking droplets of water from his silken doublet. "What manner of fish is this?" he asked, prodding it with the toe of his boot.

"A sturgeon . . . sir," John Clark answered. "The creatures have arrived a few days early this year, though they're not very reliable and don't come every year. This is a small one. Come September, many will be nine or twelve feet. Then, when they leap into your boat, you have a merry time."

"Are they useful?" Richard asked.

"Oh yes," Cisly said. "Dried, pounded, and mixed

with roe and sorrel, this one will feed a man heartily for many days. I'll teach you how,'' he added, nudging Anne gently with his elbow.

"Thank you," said Anne, but Sarah couldn't tell if she was truly grateful, since Anne's palms were pressed together in front of her mouth and her eyes were looking at the sturgeon in dismay.

"I'm glad I won't have to learn how to prepare that immense, slimy creature," Sarah whispered when she regained her seat. "The fearsome things I've seen in Virginia are already enough to last me until my hair withers gray upon my head."

Anne's laughter rang out across the river, which the midday sun had turned into a sparkling diamond necklace leading to the sea. "Oh, Sarah," she said, "not everything in Virginia is as fearsome as Indians and wild, leaping fish. Indeed, some things are quite wondrous."

"Name me one," Sarah muttered with a pout, her tone copying the slap of water against the shallop's prow.

"Turkey, my dear friend," Anne answered, laughing. "Turkey."

Chapter 10

The sun was sliding below the horizon when at last the shallop arrived at Martin's Hundred.

"It is the settlement we saw from the deck of the *Jonathan* two days ago," Anne said, as John and Cisly tethered the shallop to the wooden dock.

"Only two days ago?" groaned Sarah. "It feels like a year."

A dirt path led from the wharf to the settlement. It was just light enough to see, and after Sarah saw the few humble dwellings, the dirt track leading to the fort, and the footpaths that crisscrossed the rest of the settlement, she decided Jamestown was a civilized, miniature London compared with Martin's Hundred.

"There are five houses in the settlement," Cisly said, "plus the fort and the company compound, each with its own palisade fence for protection."

"And where is our house?" Anne asked.

Cisly pointed off to his right. "A third of a mile that way."

Sarah sucked in her breath. "You mean you won't be living right in the settlement?"

"We're not far away," Cisly said. "A five-minute walk at most."

"But it's through the . . . trees," Sarah said, her voice tiny.

Cisly stopped to shift his load onto his other shoulder. "You'll soon get used to those."

No sooner than I'll get used to Indians, Sarah thought. "Where is the Davidsons' house?" she asked then, mentioning the couple Master Boys had told her she might live with.

"Their home is on the other side of that small gully." Cisly again pointed to the right.

Sarah looked where Cisly pointed, but the trees growing along the gully blocked any sign of her new home.

A few minutes later, Master Boys was rousing Walter and Margaret Davidson and asking them if they would be willing to add Sarah to their household. They soon agreed, and John Clark and Master Jackson lifted Sarah's chests through the door of the small, wattle-and-daub dwelling.

"May I have a torch to light my bride home?" Cisly asked Walter, and all too soon Anne was hugging Sarah good-bye. Sarah clung to her friend, a lump of despair swelling her throat.

"Remember your aunt's words, Sarah," Anne whispered in her ear. " 'He shall give his angels charge over thee, to keep thee in all thy ways.' I'll visit you soon." Then she was gone, Cisly's flickering torchlight quickly becoming fainter and then disappearing, like the glimmer of a dying glowworm.

Sarah was soon settled on a pallet before the Davidsons' fireplace, which took up one entire wall of the house. She tried to close her ears to the bellowing of frogs, the howling of wolves, and the snores of Walter and Margaret, who slept in a simple frame bed across the room. From where she lay, Sarah could see the rawhide strips that supported their bedding. There was no sign of the servant Master Boys had mentioned, although a ladder led to a hole in the ceiling planks. *Perhaps he sleeps up there,* she thought.

Sarah eyed the rough, hand-hewn table, bench, and stools, the clothing hooks, the few chests that furnished the small home. She recalled the other humble dwellings she had glimpsed, the muddy track that led from the river to her new home. *'Tis a squalid place I've come to,* she thought, before she finally fell asleep.

The next morning, Margaret shook Sarah awake before the sun was up. After she had dressed, splashed water on her face, and tidied her hair, she helped with the morning meal, setting out bowls on the board and stirring the porridge, made from Indian corn.

"Sorry there's no cream for your porridge," Margaret said when she had called Walter from the field and the three of them were sitting down to breakfast.

Walter, his sloping shoulders so hunched over his porridge his chin nearly touched his wooden bowl, snorted. "There's no cow in Martin's Hundred."

"Cheated we were," Margaret added, tucking in a stray strand of her lead-gray hair, which she wore in an elaborate roll across the top of her head, a style common in the days of Elizabeth I, who was queen until 1603. "Paid the company store in Jamestown eighty pounds to bring over ten cattle a year ago." She spooned some porridge into her mouth, and for the first time Sarah really looked at her, noticing that Margaret was missing her bottom, front teeth. Those missing teeth and her gray hair made it impossible to guess the woman's age, although Sarah suspected Walter was only a few years older than Richard Kean.

"The cows came on the *Margaret* last December with the settlers for Berkley's Hundred," Walter explained. "But Abraham Piersey, the merchant in charge of the company store, sold them elsewhere for one hundred fifty pounds." He wiped his mouth with the back of his hand.

"Master Jackson wrote to the adventurers in London, he did, so I 'spect we'll be getting our cattle one of these years," Margaret said. Then she looked at the ceiling and called out, "Twig! Get your lazy bones down here."

At that moment, down the ladder came a small boy, who looked to be about eight years old. His hair, brown and lanky, straggled into eyes that were round and gray—and old. Sarah thought Twig was a good name for the urchin—his skinny legs and arms branched out in all directions like limbs on a stick figure. She smiled at him, but the only sign he gave in return was a narrowing of his eyes.

"Twig is our bondsboy," explained Margaret, spooning up some porridge for him. "He came on the *Duty* a few weeks ago with fifty other urchins plucked off the streets of London. He'll be one of your students, Sarah.

"Sit up and eat proper, boy," she snapped. "I'll not have *you* eating like an animal at my board. Teach you some manners, I will, afore you gain your freedom, though lucky it is I have twelve years to do it."

Twig lifted his head from his bowl, and his eyes narrowed further. "No one said aught 'bout my manners afore I came to this bloody place," he muttered. "In London a body was free to eat as he pleased."

"Gnawing on other's scraps and leavings when you couldn't steal money enough to buy food," sniffed Margaret.

Walter pushed himself away from the table. "Need help in the field," he said. Sarah's heart leaped, thinking Walter was speaking to her. Then she saw him looking at Twig.

"I need him for a bit," Margaret told her husband. "He'll be along in a while.

"Servants can't do any trading," Margaret explained to Sarah when Walter had gone out the door, "so I want Twig to take you to the potter's to barter for a new water jug. My old pipkin broke yesterday.

"You get busy scouring those bowls now," she told Twig, too harshly, Sarah thought. But as Margaret passed the boy, she reached out a hand and smoothed Twig's unruly thatch of hair, which looked like a nest of dried leaves.

Margaret isn't as fierce as she seems, Sarah told herself, and rose to help Twig clear the board and scrub the bowls and bake kettle.

"What is your real name, Twig?" Sarah asked a short time later, pleased to find she was not tongue-tied with the child.

"Just Twig," he muttered, shutting the palisade gate behind them and leading Sarah past the clucking hens pecking for beetles in the garden.

"Have you no family name—or even a different given name?"

"Just Twig."

"But what did your mother and father call you?"

Twig fixed a fierce gaze on Sarah. "Never had a father or a mum."

Poor Twig, Sarah thought, looking away to where Walter was walking slowly through a small field on the river side of the dwelling. He had a basket over his arm, and beside each bare mound of soil that warted from the ground, he dropped a small plant.

"Master Davidson's tobacco field," Twig said. "I help the master stick the cursed plants into the hills," he added, leading Sarah toward the gully behind the Davidsons'. A worn path ambled down through some trees, past an immense maple, and some stones led across the stream to the far side.

"Good for climbin'," Twig said, with a jerk of his

60

head toward the maple. He looked at Sarah, his eyebrows raised in an unspoken suggestion.

Sarah hesitated. The tree reminded her of the oak that grew near her old home in London. Aunt Mary had told her proper girls didn't climb trees, but Sarah had continued to sit among its branches until the day they sailed for Virginia. She looked back toward the house. There were no windows on this side, and the palisade wall was nearly as high as the roof. She nodded, set the basket of eggs Margaret had given her for barter on the ground, then looping her skirts over her arm, she scampered up the maple behind Twig. Moments later, they were sitting on neighboring branches high above the ground, looking down at Martin's Hundred.

Chapter 11

"Who lives there?" Sarah asked, pointing through the maple leaves to a dwelling across the gully, a large tree shading its wattle-fenced yard.

"Master Boys's place," Twig stated.

Sarah looked past the Boyses' to a cluster of buildings surrounded by a partially completed palisade.

"The company compound," Twig said, seeing where she looked. "This end is the byre, what's waitin' for those cows. That part in the middle is the longhouse where the unmarried men sleep. That's the store at t'other end there."

A lone, bald-headed man was working beside a small shed near a pond at the far end of the compound. "Master James," said Twig. "The potter."

"How many folk live in the settlement?" Sarah asked then.

"I heard Walter say thirty, however many that be."

"Only thirty people! Why, there were nearly two hundred people on the *Jonathan*. And all of London has over two hundred thousand. It will be strange to live among so few." She squirmed on her branch, thought how wonderful it was to be sitting among leaves again, then asked, "And how many people in the entire Hundred?"

"How should I know?" the boy snapped.

For a moment, Sarah was shocked by Twig's rudeness, but then she guessed the reason for it. "Can you count, Twig?" she asked.

He shook his head no.

"Well, you shall learn. That is why I've come: to teach you and any other indentured children in Martin's Hundred."

"No need to learn," Twig said. "Soon's I can I'm gonna run away and go back to London."

Sarah didn't know what to say, since she felt the same way, so she quickly thought of a new subject.

"Are there many Indians hereabouts, Twig?"

At this question, a gleam came into Twig's eyes. "Aye. They come 'ere real regular-like."

Sarah dug her tattered fingernails into the bark beside her. "Are they . . . fierce?" she asked, hoping Twig wouldn't notice how upset she felt at the thought of Indians lurking about the settlement.

"Them Injuns'll scalp ya afore you've a chance to tell 'em good day," he said solemnly. "Only last week I ran into a wicked 'un over by Jacob Howe's. He tried to scalp me, but I wiggled and kicked so much, he botched it. Did bite off me little finger though," he said, thrusting his hand under Sarah's nose.

Most of the little finger on his left hand was missing, and Sarah felt faint for a moment and clutched more tightly at the trunk of the maple. Then she saw the glint in Twig's eye and realized the finger had been missing longer than a week.

"You crafty noddy!" she exclaimed, giving the boy, sitting on his nearby branch, a light rap on the head.

For the first time, Twig smiled—a wide, toothy smile.

The old look in his eyes vanished, and he became the teasing child he truly was.

"How did you lose your finger? The truth now or I shall give you a real clout."

"In truth, 'twas bit off," he answered, plucking a maple leaf and slowly shredding it. "Baggie Willie bit it off when we was tusslin' over a gent's pocket watch afore I was snatched up and hauled to Virginia."

"And where would the likes of you get a gentleman's pocket watch?"

"Lifted it."

Sarah gasped, much to the rascal's delight. "It wouldn't be a good idea to be so light-fingered in Virginia," she scolded, "lest you want to find yourself in the stocks."

Twig grinned at Sarah. "Not much booty ta lift, no place ta fence the booty, and no money ta get fer it either. Not one of those blokes has two farthin's to jingle in 'is pocket," he said, waving a hand toward the people digging in the nearby field and those building the new company barn on the far side of the fort.

The fort, with its single large building and two small sheds, stood about a hundred yards away, surrounded by a palisade taller than a man's head. This palisade was not a triangle, like the palisade at Jamestown, but a rectangle. On the river side of the palisade, at the corner nearest Sarah, sat a gun platform, and Sarah saw the maw of a cannon. A man stood near the cannon, keeping watch downriver. *No doubt guarding against Spanish ships,* Sarah thought.

A watchtower stood on the other corner, the one nearest the thick forest. Again a man stood watch, only this time he watched the trees. *For Indians?* Sarah wondered.

At that moment a man passed through the gate in the center of the western wall of the palisade. He carried a matchlock musket; a sword hung at his side. He was encased in armor, his head topped by a close helmet with only a slit for his eyes and a few holes near his nose. It already was a warm day, and Sarah couldn't imagine how he could breathe, for her gown seemed glued to her skin. She envied Twig, who ran around in loose breeches and sleeveless canvas jerkin, feet and legs bare.

The man started to march down the muddy track before the fort. There was something familiar about the strutting step, and Sarah realized it was Richard Kean.

One by one the people working on the barn and in the tobacco field raised their heads to look toward Richard. Some stood with their mouths open. Some turned away, their shoulders shaking in mirth.

Sarah was wondering what the people found so amusing, when she noticed Twig gaping at the sight of Richard in his armor.

"Be that the new lieutenant?" he asked, his voice full of awe.

"Aye."

"P'rhaps I will be a soldier when I am man-grown," he confided. "I think t'would be even more fun than bein' a sailor."

"It's certainly a better career than thief," Sarah chided. Twig looked at her from the corner of his eye and swung his legs in an unruffled way. "But, I think," Sarah added, "strutting about in the hot Virginia sun, swathed in a coat of metal and feeling like a bake kettle hung above the flames, doesn't look like much fun.

"Come now. We best get that pipkin Mistress Davidson wants, before Walter comes looking for you with fire in his eye."

Sarah eased herself off her branch and began to climb down the tree. With a groan, Twig followed.

Chapter 12

They had finished cleaning up after the evening meal of raccoon, a meat that Sarah thought tasted much like lamb. The sun had set, and the day's breeze had died. The Davidsons sat by the fireplace, watching the smoldering coals and smoking their clay pipes. Twig, too, had his own small pipe and sat puffing like a chimney.

Sarah remembered reading in his *Counter Blaste* that King James thought smoking "a custom loathsome to the eye, hateful to the nose, harmful to the brain, dangerous to the lungs." Sarah secretly agreed with the king, but she thought she was the only one in Martin's Hundred, perhaps in all of Virginia, to do so. It seemed all the other people in the settlement smoked, breathed, grew, and dreamed tobacco. The weed was so prized that the colonists didn't bother to grow their own corn, instead trading for it with the Indians.

A knock at the open door interrupted her thoughts.

"My wife has missed her friend, so we've come for a visit," Cisly said. "We were too busy with work to come before." He handed Margaret a bunch of early wild onions, their bulbs the size of Sarah's tiniest fingernail.

Sarah took Anne's newly blistered hands and drew her aside. "It seems a year, not a week, since I saw you last," she told her friend, studying Anne's face before adding, "And is Cisly the good man you hoped to find?"

"Aye," Anne said, and she laughed a quiet laugh, her glance fluttered toward Cisly, and her sunburned face became even redder, before breaking into a small, secret smile that told of things Sarah had yet to learn.

What was it like, Sarah wondered, to be married? To be held in a man's arms? Sarah's mother had died before Sarah was old enough to be told such things. Aunt Mary had had no knowledge to share. Sarah ached to ask Anne, but couldn't find the courage.

"And you?" Anne asked. "Are things going well with you?"

"I teach three pupils each morning," Sarah said. "In the afternoons I help Margaret around the house. She said I won't have to do hard labor during the summer heat until I'm seasoned and used to this weather. And she said women rarely do field work. I'm grateful for that, for even with the easy work, moisture runs down my body in rivulets and my head pounds as though a wee urchin inside it is beating a hammer against my skull. By next summer, when I'm seasoned, I'll be home in England."

"Then, within a year, you'll earn enough from tutoring to pay your fare home?" said Anne quietly, her voice shaded with disappointment.

Sarah gasped and covered her mouth with her hand, causing the others in the room to look at them.

"What is it?" Anne asked.

"I never asked Master Boys or Master Jackson how much I'll earn from my tutoring," Sarah whispered.

"Oh, Sarah." Anne shook her head. "You had best

find out, else how can you know for certain when you'll be sailing home?"

"I'll ask tomorrow."

"I hope it's only one pound a year," Anne said with a smile. "Then I'll have you with me forever. Now, let's join the others."

"I saw Richard my first day here," Sarah told Anne quietly, as they started toward the fireplace where the others were seated. "He was dressed in armor and the people were laughing at him."

"He must be worrying about the Indians, that's why the armor. But I don't know why the people were laughing. Perhaps we can ask Walter."

The two girls were seating themselves on stools when another knock came at the door, and who should be waiting but Richard himself.

"I hope I'm not intruding," he said, looking about.

"Not at all," announced Walter, drawing him into the room.

Sarah squeezed Anne's hand. Anne shrugged, as though to say it bothered her not at all to be around Richard.

Soon the glow of Richard's pipe added its light to the glow of the fire and to that of the pine knot set across the room. Twig crept off into a corner, his eyes large with wonder at the nearness of his new idol.

"You're not wearing your armor, lieutenant," said Walter. Sarah knew Walter to be a sober man, so she told herself she only imagined hearing a chuckle in his voice.

"I've taken to wearing it only when I go into the forest or when I know the natives are expected in the settlement," Richard answered. "Indeed, armor is punishingly hot and cumbersome in this climate. Perhaps I'll take an Indian arrow without it, but wearing it I would surely die of the heat." He drew on his pipe before continuing. "Although eighty thousand acres is a large area to protect, and we are short of muskets, few people live outside the town itself. And, fortunately, the natives seem rather docile. Perhaps knowing that I'm a professional soldier willing to punish them for their villainies is keeping them peaceful," he added, flicking a speck of ash from his broadcloth breeches.

Cisly lifted his head as though to disagree, but a look from Anne held him quiet. Instead, he laughed softly and said, "Ever since Chief Powhatan died in 1618 and Opechancanough made himself head werowance, the Powhatan tribes have been friendly. They come and go as they please."

"A dangerous situation," announced Richard, "and one I hope to correct." A log fell, and tumbling sparks snapped at each other in the gloom.

"So, we are overly trusting . . ." said Cisly, a note of challenge in his voice. Sarah held her breath, hoping the men wouldn't quarrel about how to deal with the Indians. It was the first chance she'd had to visit with Anne, and she didn't want anything to spoil it.

"Sarah, do you know who lives across the gully near this house?" asked Anne quickly, interrupting the tense moment and allowing Sarah to breathe again.

"Yes." Sarah recalled the folk she had met in the past week. "The Boys, the Cumbers, the Jacksons, the Snows, and the company servants, though I've yet to meet most of the latter."

"Nay, I mean the other direction."

"Who, Anne? Though I doubt I know them."

"But you do," said Cisly. " 'Tis Jacob Howe and Rose."

It was only then that Sarah recalled Twig telling her he had met his finger-biting Indian near the home of Jacob Howe.

The mention of Rose and Jacob brought on a bout

of laughter, in which Margaret and Walter couldn't join until the others had wiped their eyes and quieted enough to tell them what was so funny. Even Richard smiled a bit.

"We stopped by the Howes' on our way here," explained Anne. "Cisly told me they lived hereabouts, and I was curious to see how Rose was getting on. I knew you'd be curious to hear, too," she added.

Walter leaned forward and hucked a gob of spit into the fire, where it sizzled and danced before vanishing.

Sarah scooted her chair farther away from the flames. "And how are the Howes getting on?" she said, thinking of Rose on the day she was wed, trailing dazedly after Jacob.

"It's difficult to tell," Anne told her. "Jacob said only a few words, Rose none at all." She shook her head. "Rose didn't seem the brazen hussy she was on the ship."

"I suspect Rose wishes she had chosen Hugh," interrupted Cisly, "for if the Howe dwelling were a chicken yard and Jacob its scrawny rooster, the sun would rise promptly when he cock-a-doodle-dooed. As puny as he is, I suspect it would be dangerous to disobey Jacob."

Poor Rose, thought Sarah. She almost wished she had let the woman steal Aunt Mary's favorite shawl.

The talk of Rose and Jacob had turned their thoughts away from the Indians, and more pleasant conversation followed. As darkness crept around the dwelling, they spoke of finishing the church and the expected arrival of William Harwood, the new head of Martin's Hundred. The frogs commenced their evening bellow, and it was a bellow, for the frogs of Virginia were enormous. Some, when spread-legged, were longer than Sarah's forearm. Finally, a whippoorwill called, and everyone fell quiet.

At length, Richard's voice split the stillness. "I saw

two graves near the gully as I approached,'' he said to Margaret.

Sarah had also noticed the graves, but had been afraid to mention them. She watched now as Margaret drew herself straighter on her stool. For his part, Walter seemed to grow smaller, though it seemed impossible for a man so large. Margaret drew breath.

''It is the resting place of our two daughters. They were taken by the fever last summer. Only eleven and thirteen years they were.'' Margaret's calloused hand fluttered toward her face, but then reached up and smoothed her hair. It was too dark to see clearly, but Sarah thought she saw a tear glisten on Margaret's cheek.

Judging from the age of Margaret's daughters, Sarah decided the woman could not be much more than thirty, only a few years older than Aunt Mary. The thought of her aunt's body sliding into the sea, of her mother and father buried on the other side of the world, flashed into Sarah's mind. Sarah knew the pain that came from losing those you love, and her heart ached for Margaret, yet she felt a twinge of envy, because, though dead, Margaret's loved ones were still near.

''It is a raw, harsh land we've come to,'' Margaret said then. ''And we are the only barrier of civilization.''

Richard emptied his pipe and rose to his feet. As he took his leave, Sarah saw him gently lay his hand on Margaret's shoulder.

Chapter 13

It had rained during the night. The June sun had sucked the moisture from the damp earth and draped the morning with a steamy veil. Sarah, seated on her favorite branch, leaned her head against the trunk of the maple, hearing again in her head the words Master Boys had spoken only moments before.

"Why, we assumed your room and board would be payment for your tutoring," Master Boys had said, tugging at his lower lip.

Speaking to his shirtfront, Sarah managed to explain that she needed to earn her return fare to England. The man kicked the toe of his boot into the dust and thought a while. "I'm sorry you don't wish to stay in Virginia," he said finally. "I'll see if Master Jackson will agree to pay you ten pounds a year for each child you tutor."

Ten pounds! With three pupils, at the end of a year Sarah would have thirty pounds, more than enough money for her fare. She was about to thank Master Boys for his generous offer when he added, "That's pounds of tobacco, not currency. As you may have learned, there is little money in Virginia."

The breath went out of Sarah. Ten pounds of tobacco per pupil per year? It had cost Cisly one hundred and twenty pounds of tobacco to pay Anne's fare. Why, at that rate it would be four years before she earned enough money to go home.

It had taken Sarah a week to find the courage to approach Master Boys to ask about her wages. Now, it took an even greater effort to look him in the face and thank him. But she managed, because even a few pounds of tobacco were more wages than they had planned to give her. After, she had fled up the maple.

Now she sat looking down on Martin's Hundred as it lay steaming in the morning sun, kicking her legs angrily and longing to tell Anne of her disappointment. Since she didn't tutor Dick, Will, and Twig on Sunday, she would go visit Anne, she decided. But she didn't relish the thought of making her first journey into the forest alone, so she climbed down the tree and went in search of Twig.

"Nay," Twig replied. "I can't take ya. I'm off to gig for turtles. Giggin' is best after a rain." With his thumb, he tested the sharpness of the barbed point he'd tied to a stick, and gave Sarah a sly look. "Scared to walk in the woods are ya?"

Sarah pulled a face at him. "I am not," she fibbed. "I'm quite content to go alone."

"Best tell Margaret where yer goin'," Twig said. "She'll need to know what way to come searchin' for yer scalped pate when ya don't come back." He grinned at Sarah and scampered off to probe muddy streams with his stick until he pierced a turtle shell.

It was nearly midday before Sarah had gathered enough courage to go on her way, first slinging a basket over her arm for the wild strawberries Margaret had asked her to pick.

She followed the path into the trees, then stopped and listened. The sound of the forest was nearly deafening to Sarah's English ears. She half expected to hear the growl of a bear or the scream of an Indian, but the gnats buzzed about her head and the birds gave raucous calls from the treetops, as though to drown any noise that might hint of danger.

Sarah jumped when a red bird that Walter called a cardinal piped a few notes at her. But then a longing for home filled her. *Oh,* she thought, *it sounds like the English nightingale that used to sing outside my window. So even if it is dressed in the red robes of a cardinal, I'll call it a Virginia nightingale.*

The bird darted away, and Sarah became aware of the moisture oozing between her breasts and under her arms. "It's too hot for any sensible bear to be out," she reassured herself, and went forward, slowly at first, then more quickly as her confidence grew.

In a few minutes she came upon a fallen white oak lying across a streambed, the oak Anne had told her marked the corner of their property. Sarah felt something inside her go soft, and she realized she had been more frightened than she knew. Then the smell of crushed strawberries underfoot reminded her of the empty basket, which she soon filled to overflowing.

Moments later Sarah smelled smoke and saw the stake palisade surrounding Anne's house. The thwack of an ax told her Cisly was nearby. Moments later, his white shirt stained with sweat, his freckles dripping, he greeted Sarah fondly, then went back to his labors, leaving Anne and Sarah to visit.

Anne's eyes shone with pride as she showed Sarah around her home. "It's as humble as any other house in Martin's Hundred," Anne said.

"But it's special, because it's yours," Sarah told her.

"This was my mother's," Anne said, suddenly shy, as she showed Sarah the pewter charger used to carry food to the table. "And this," she explained, holding out a table knife encrusted with silver, "belonged to Cisly's grandfather. Isn't it lovely?"

"Yes, it is. And it's the only table knife I've seen in Martin's Hundred."

Taking down a yellow-glazed dish, Anne filled it with some of the strawberries Sarah offered. "Now come," she ordered. "Let's go outside and sit in the shade to eat these plump berries."

The girls found a spot under a tree where the breeze was filled with the scent of laurel blossoms. It was not enough of a breeze, though, to discourage the biting gnats from flying up their noses and into their ears.

"Did you ask the burgesses about your wages, Sarah?" Anne asked, when they were seated and had gossiped for a while.

Sarah told Anne of her conversation with Master Boys. "Oh, Anne," she said, drawing the back of her hand across her eyes, "it will be four years before I earn my fare. I don't think I can bear to live in this land that long."

A nearby mockingbird flicked its tail from side to side in time with its song, as if taunting Sarah.

Anne studied the bird, then her friend. "Is it really so terrible here?" she asked.

Sarah looked down at her hands with their ragged fingernails. "Yes," she said in a small voice. "Though I haven't starved to death, and have yet to find myself close enough to an Indian to smell the bear grease I've heard they wear in their hair, I've never worked so hard in all my years." She raised her hands and flapped them before her face to fan herself. "And the heat is brutal!"

"You're right about the work and the heat. But I confess, I'm glad you'll be staying in Virginia for some time yet, although if many more indentured children come, you'll earn your fare quickly."

"That's true," said Sarah, raising her head. "If I had

ten more pupils, I'd have enough tobacco within the year. But I can't count on that. Isn't there any other way?''

Anne puffed up her cheeks, then slowly blew out the air. ''I'll probably regret sharing this with you, but you can sell soap ashes to earn money.''

Sarah looked at Anne doubtfully. ''Soap ashes? Where, pray tell, do I get soap ashes to sell?''

''You make them, of course. You burn wood and collect the ashes. You deliver the ashes to the company store in Jamestown, which sends them to England to be made into soap. A hundred weight brings six to eight shillings.'' Anne raised a finger. ''Of course you'll need thousands of pounds of soap ashes, along with a year's tutoring wages, to earn you your fare, but it's a start.''

Sarah groaned. ''It's hopeless.''

''Then perhaps you better claim that headright and plant your own tobacco,'' Anne snapped.

Startled, Sarah looked at Anne. Her friend was probably tired of hearing her complain, she realized, just as Anne clapped her hands and said, ''I know! Claim your land, Sarah. Burn the trees on it to make soap ashes, and plant tobacco on the cleared spaces.''

Sarah jumped to her feet. ''Mistress Mills, you are a dreamer. How could I cut the trees to burn them?'' She waved her arms at the forest surrounding them. ''These trees are thicker than I am tall.''

Anne shook her head. ''You don't cut down the trees, you simply take off a strip of bark all the way round the trunk. It's called girdling. A girdled tree dies. When it's dead, you burn it. Even before the trees are dry enough to burn, you can plant between them.''

Sarah stared at Anne in astonishment. ''How do you know this?'' she asked, trying to ignore the tiny spark of excitement that was glowing within her.

Anne blushed, waving her skirts to cool her legs.

76

"Cisly," she said simply. "He's teaching me everything he's learned about living here." She leaned her head toward the sound of Cisly's ax. "That's what he's doing now. Girdling."

Anne stood up, smoothing her skirt and straightening her cap. "It's something to think about, Sarah. And now it's time to begin the evening meal. Will you stay?"

"No," Sarah answered, thoughts of soap ashes and tobacco and girdled trees all tumbling about in her head. "I told Margaret I'd be back to help her. I didn't realize we'd chatted away the afternoon."

Just then Cisly strode up carrying an odd-looking creature that reminded Sarah of a large rat with scraggly hair. It was curled up tight except for its tail, which Cisly held. When he reached them, he carefully laid the animal, which he called a possum, on the ground.

"Is it dead?" asked Anne, when the possum didn't move.

"No," said Cisly, "just playing dead." With a stick he gingerly unrolled the animal enough to see its belly.

"Why, it has a pocket," exclaimed Anne. "What use could it have for such a thing?"

"It's a rich beastie and needs a purse to hide its wealth," teased Cisly.

"You jest," laughed Anne.

"I jest," agreed Cisly. "But it will make a tasty supper."

A shadow passed over Anne's face. "If we're going to make a meal of the fellow, I wish I'd never made his acquaintance."

"You're too softhearted, my sweet," Cisly said. "Come winter, when hunger pains your innards and makes you cry for food, you'll think once again of this possum."

At that moment something moved near the stomach

of the creature; a small head peeped out of the pocket and squinted around at the world.

"Look, Cisly!" cried Anne. "It's a pouch for carrying the young."

"Why, so it seems," agreed Cisly, though Sarah suspected he knew it all along.

"Now, indeed, we'll not have it for our supper," Anne stated firmly.

"Aye," said Cisly. He prodded it gently with his stick. The animal once again curled into a tight bundle, refusing to move. Not until Cisly started back toward his ax, and Anne and Sarah were waving farewell, did it rise to its feet and scurry off into the trees.

Sarah laughed as she watched it disappear. Indeed, there were strange sights in Virginia. An animal with a pocket. But was it any stranger than the thought of her making soap ashes or girdling trees?

Chapter 14

The forest seemed more familiar to Sarah as she started toward home, the noises less strange, when suddenly from behind her came menacing snuffles and grunts. Her stomach churning, Sarah turned to see nothing but the waggle of bushes. The noise came nearer, and Sarah fled, the sound of furious squealing in her ears.

Headlong she raced, tripping over the hem of her gown and spilling strawberries, her heart thudding so hard in her chest she heard it echo inside her skull.

Sarah had run through a small clearing and was again entering the woods when the figure of an Indian appeared before her. She screamed as the man's wide-flung arms reached out to grab her.

Sarah had heard that people do strange things in times of danger, and, now, she found this to be true, for she promptly raised her arms to tuck any trailing wisps of hair under her cap. *If he can't see my hair, he'll not want my scalp,* she told herself crazily.

Even as she did so, Sarah's frightened mind noticed that the yellow-painted, foul-smelling native was dressed in the breeches and shirt of an Englishman. *What white man did you murder for your dress, hea-*

then? she wondered. Then she noticed something familiar about his eyes. He spoke.

"Mistress Douglas," he said. "It's John Clark."

Sarah pushed herself away from the man. *John Clark? The servant who sailed downriver with us and clouted the monster fish?* She peered into the man's face, something she never would have been able to do under ordinary circumstances.

"My apologies, mistress," he continued. "I must look frightening to a young lady not used to the ways of native Virginia."

Suddenly, knowing no harm would come to her, Sarah's knees went watery and she sank down on a rotted log behind her.

"I *am* sorry," John repeated. "And if you don't want an infestation of red worms, you best rise from that log."

Sarah leaped to her feet. After a moment she regained her breath and asked timidly, "What is that . . . that stuff you wear on your skin?"

"It's an Indian ointment made from bear oil, puccoon roots and angelica, and used to keep off the long-tailed biting gnats." He waved his arm at the cloud of muskeets swarming about Sarah's head. "You'd be wise to wear it yourself lest all your blood be sucked dry by the creatures."

Sarah sniffed, then mumbled, "I've no wish to smell like a dead cow."

"Perhaps the young lady would feel more kindly toward the ointment if she knew it also keeps the skin soft as a babe's bottom," John said, the gold flecks in his eyes lighting up with a mischievous glint.

Sarah had no time to blush at his comment, for suddenly, from behind her, came the same grunts and snuffles that had sent her flying through the trees. Her scream sent the birds rocketing from their branches.

"Ah," said John, "I thought you were moving rather quickly through the trees when we met. Look," he said, pointing, "it's one of the Martin's Hundred swine turned loose to forage on mast."

Out of the bush waddled a ponderous sow followed by a litter of piglets, all snuffling and grunting as they snouted along the ground searching for nuts and acorns.

"Only a sow." Sarah sighed, her heart settling back where it belonged. "I needn't have run after all."

"You were wise to keep your distance." John motioned Sarah away. "A sow with piglets can be a vicious beast."

"Rawhunt," he called then, and from out of the trees, where he must have been standing all the while, stepped a true son of Virginia. Like the Indian of Jamestown, one side of his head was shaved, and he wore only an apron of animal skin around his middle. A dead rat swung by its tail from a hole in his right earlobe. His body, too, was painted yellow and gave off a powerful odor.

"This is Mistress Sarah Douglas," John told the Indian. "She is new to the settlement, and it's plain she'll need looking after. Between us, we can make sure she comes to no harm."

Sarah's heart almost halted. *An Indian? Horrors!* Surely this was not the angel Aunt Mary had said would watch over her.

Rawhunt said something in his native Algonquian tongue.

"What did he say?" Sarah asked John in a whisper.

"He said you are near the age of his youngest sister and he would be pleased to watch over you whenever he is near."

Sarah's hands shook as she and John bent to fill her basket again. She could feel the Indian's eyes on her, and the back of her neck prickled.

81

"The fishing went well today," John said a while later, as he and the Indian led her through the trees to the palisade gate of the Davidsons'. "Perhaps Mistress Davidson would like some herring for the evening meal."

"I'm sure she would," Sarah mumbled, "if you have some to spare. You . . . you must be a good fisherman," she stammered, seeing the large string of fish John uncovered in the basket Rawhunt carried.

At that moment Margaret came through the palisade gate. "He is a hopeless fisherman," she said with a laugh, having overheard.

John nodded. "I am." He tilted his head toward Rawhunt. "My friend here knows the ways of the water and is willing to teach me what he knows." He handed the fish to Margaret.

"I thank you," she said. "Do you have enough for Mistress Boys?"

"Aye. More than enough."

"I trust Hannah is well," Margaret said. "Give her my greetings."

John nodded. After he and Rawhunt had disappeared around the corner of the palisade, Sarah asked. "Who is Hannah? I know John Clark is the Boyses' servant, but Mistress Boys's name isn't Hannah."

Margaret plucked a strawberry from Sarah's basket. "Hannah is John's wife. She's servant to the Boys, same as him. A hearty girl she is. Came on the *Bona Nova* last December and wed John in Jamestown."

"How old is she?" asked Sarah.

Margaret shook her head. "Four years older than John, I believe, which would make her around twenty-four." She gave Sarah a knowing look. "Not too old to be a friend to you.

"Come now," she said abruptly. "We'll put the herring out to dry. Twig caught a large turtle for our evening meal. It's roasting in the coals."

"I've never eaten turtle."

"It's delicious. You'll like it."

I hope you're right, Sarah thought, wondering as she closed the palisade gate behind them what part of a turtle one ate, and wondering, too, if she would ever again go into the forest, knowing Rawhunt might be watching her.

⬡⬡⬡

Chapter 15

The July air hung stagnant over Martin's Hundred. Hot as it was, Sarah leaned into the smoke of her fire to escape the biting flies. Burning elm to make soap ashes was a miserable way to spend a Sunday, but Sarah had decided to take some of Anne's advice, because, after two months in Virginia, she still dreamed of returning to England.

Twig was somewhere nearby setting his own small fires to smoke hares out of hollow trees. Sarah was glad he'd come. She still didn't like being alone in the forest. She often saw gray shadows moving silently through the trees. Once she stumbled upon Rawhunt as she walked home from picking cherries, and her skin prickled, for she suspected he had been spying on her. John Clark wasn't with him. She'd seen little of John since the day she first met Rawhunt, and Sarah had yet to meet John's wife.

With a loud whooping, Twig appeared out of the trees. "Look here, Sarah," he cried. "I caught me four hares. Aren't they fine ones now?"

"That they are. Margaret will be pleased."

"And Baggie Willie 'ud be most jealous if he knew. I bet he's fingerin' a gent's purse right this minute so he can buy hisself some food." He scratched at his tangled brown thatch. "And here in Virginia I stepped out my door but a few minutes past and here I be— with four fat beasts fer our supper." He hefted the furry, brown corpses proudly, dipping their long, limp ears into the dirt.

"You sound content with your life," Sarah said. "Are you no longer thinking of running off to England?" She jabbed at the smoldering wood with a stick, distressed that Twig might be giving up his plans to return to England. She felt betrayed.

"I've decided to wait a bit and see," Twig said. "It's . . . it's . . . nice to have a home."

Aye, a home in England, Sarah thought, *where your bones don't melt in summer and savages don't spy on you.* But she said nothing to Twig. "I have an idea," she said then. "I haven't seen Rose, and though we're not friends, I'm curious to learn how she's getting along. The Howes live near these woods. Why don't we take her one of your fine hares?"

Twig nibbled at his lower lip a moment. Then he swabbed a grimy hand at a runnel of sweat trickling down his cheek and nodded. "I've yet to meet Mistress Howe, so I shall go. But I hope we'll not see Master Howe. He looks much like a cattail goin' ta seed."

Sarah, too, hoped she didn't see Jacob. She had met more men the past few months than she had met in her lifetime, but she still was not easy with strange ones. Even visiting Rose would take courage, but with Twig's company, she felt brave enough to try.

Sarah banked the fire carefully, for there had been little rain that summer. Twig hung three of his hares from a branch of a tall sycamore, away from hungry scavengers, and they set off through the trees.

"Hallo-o-o," Twig called when the house came into sight. Opening the palisade gate, they stepped through.

Rose stood with her back to them, hoeing a scraggly garden. She glanced at them over her shoulder, then went back to her work.

Jacob sat on the nearby doorstep, a live pigeon in his lap. He pierced the bird's lower eyelid, inserted a thread, and drew the lid up and over the eye, tying it to keep the eye closed.

At the sight, Sarah felt as though she had been punched in the stomach. Forgetting her shyness around strange men, she blurted, "What are you doing?"

Only then did Jacob look up. "Making decoys," he snapped, his loose tufts of hair bobbing. "What do you want, missy?"

"We ... we ... came to see Rose," Sarah stammered. "And to bring you this." She reached behind her, to where Twig had retreated, and took the hare from his hand, feeling him pressed against her as though behind a sheltering tree. "Twig made a fine catch today." She held the hare out toward Jacob, who grabbed it. Taking up a knife from beside him on the step, he swiftly gutted the animal. Then, as he made a few more cuts and yanked off the skin, much as a mother pulls off her child's shirt, he whistled. Rose turned, and when Jacob beckoned, she laid down her hoe and shuffled toward them.

Jacob whistled again, and Rose picked up her skirt and ran. When she approached the porch, Jacob held out the skinned hare. "Our supper," he said in his thin, nasal voice, before Rose even had the chance to say hello.

"Hello, Rose," Sarah said, as the woman took the shiny, pink carcass from Jacob.

Rose looked at her, her eyes empty. "I heard you were in Martin's Hundred," she said flatly.

Sarah drew Twig around in front of her. "This is Mistress Howe, Twig."

Both Rose and Twig gasped, and the color fled their cheeks. Jacob looked sharply at Rose. She attempted a smile, but it was a poor one that pulled her pale lips against her yellowed teeth. "It's Twig of the streets," she explained, as Twig backed against Sarah's skirts, as though fearing for his life. "Twig and me know each other—from London," she said, her gaze flitting about from person to person. "Now I best be fixin' this hare." She glanced toward her husband, then scurried into the house.

Together, Sarah and Twig took a couple of steps backward. "I . . . I must get back to my fire," she said. "I'm making . . . soap . . . ashes," she finished lamely.

It was not until they were safely beside Sarah's fire again that the color returned to Twig's cheeks.

"Did you know Rose well in London?" Sarah asked then.

"She lived on the street, same as me. I saw her near every day."

"On the street? You mean she had no home?"

Twig shrugged.

"Were you friends?"

"Never!" Twig fairly spat the word. "Why, she's a . . . she's a . . ."

"A what?"

Twig shook his head. "Nothin'," he said, and bent to scoop ashes into a basket.

It would be many months before Sarah could pry more out of him.

∽∽∽
Chapter 16

The woman peered at Sarah. "Be *you* the new *tutor?*" she asked, her smile bringing a sparkle to her eyes and making Sarah forget that she bellowed some words, forget the plainness of her solid, square face, the scattered hairs sprouting on an upper lip glistening with sweat in the August heat, a heat that seemed to wind itself around Sarah like a heavy, steaming blanket.

A few days before, the *Francis Bonaventure* had sailed upriver. The settlement was expecting the arrival of William Harwood, the head of the hundred, so immediately Richard and Master Jackson had followed in the shallop. If Harwood were not aboard the *Bonaventure,* perhaps there would be, instead, a cow or two for Martin's Hundred.

Now, the people of the settlement had gathered at the shore to wait for the shallop's return. It was the first time so many had come together since Sarah's arrival, a few, even, from outlying sites. Most were huddled in small groups visiting with those they hadn't seen for a time. Some, Sarah had never seen at all: Thomas and Matilda Jones, Robert Adams, Augustine and Winnifred

Leak, Henry Eliott, and others. It was also the first time she had seen the woman who spoke to her now.

Sarah nodded, pushing back the corkscrews of unruly hair that always seemed to be sticking to her damp face. "Yes, I'm the new tutor."

"Then you're the one John rescued from the dreaded *swine* a few weeks ago."

Sarah looked to see if the woman was teasing her, but her look was concerned and friendly. At that moment Margaret bustled over and said, "Hannah, how have you been keeping?" and Sarah realized this was John Clark's wife.

As Hannah and Margaret talked, Sarah wondered why John had chosen Hannah for his wife, since they seemed very different from each other. Margaret had told her they married the day after Hannah's arrival, so she assumed their union occurred in much the same way as Anne and Cisly's.

"Come and share our evening meal after," Margaret told Hannah. "Cisly and Anne Mills are coming too." She waved at John, standing nearby with Rawhunt, who had a stuffed hawk with widespread wings upon his head in honor of the occasion. Another Indian, Camohan, was with them. Although the Indians often wandered about the settlement, trading game for trinkets, or for weapons and ammunition if they could find someone willing to break the rules, it still made Sarah shiver just to look at them.

Leaving his native friends, John joined them. Hannah greeted her husband with a proud smile. "Did you know John carved a *chair* as a welcoming *gift* for Master Harwood?" she said to Sarah. "John has a *fine* hand for making furniture."

"Aye," said Margaret. "He's a much better furniture maker than he is a fisherman."

Hannah covered a giggle with a seamed hand ingrained with dirt and hardened with callouses. Sarah looked down at her own hands and realized they were no better. Not only did she still have the ragged nails Aunt Mary used to scold her for, but now she also had callouses, as well as burns and scars from her soap-ash fires.

"I *should* be better at making furniture," John said. "I've been a fisherman for only a few months, but I apprenticed with a joiner for two years."

"I didn't know that," said Hannah, reminding Sarah again of how quickly the couple had wed and how little they must have known each other beforehand. "I thought you were in *school* when you weren't working on your father's *land*."

"When I was twelve, my father decided I'd had enough of books and set me to learn woodworking," John explained, grinding the heel of his boot into the dirt. "I enjoyed it, but I missed my studies and went about with such a long face my father gave in and sent me back to school. I was there until I was sixteen, when he died."

Sarah studied John from under her eyelashes. His dark brown hair had a slight curl, his handsome face a gentle look about it, despite the scar on his right cheek. There was none of Richard Kean's haughtiness in his eyes. He is the older brother I wish I had, Sarah thought. She gathered her courage and asked him, "What brought you to Virginia?"

"Naturally, my oldest brother took over the family farm," John said, now rocking back and forth on his heels. "For a few years I worked as a tenant farmer for him. But I wanted my own land, and I knew I wouldn't get it in England. Not wanting to be indebted to my brother for my fare and my provisions, I indentured myself, and at age nineteen, came to Virginia."

Sarah turned her gaze on Hannah. "And you?" she asked. "What brought you to Virginia?"

Hannah gave a loud snort of laughter. "Me father shipped me off, saying I 'ud *never* find a husband in England. I 'ud at least be of some use in Virginia as an indentured servant, he told me, and would no longer be a *burden* on the family." Pain flickered briefly in Hannah's brown eyes before she said, "He 'ud have a *fit*, he would, if he knew I had caught me a *fine* husband the day after I arrived." She grinned at John.

John looked rather uncomfortable with the attention, but nevertheless smiled back at his wife and said, "I'm grateful your father sent you to the New World."

It was Hannah's turn to flush and smile down at her bare toes.

At that moment a cry went up, and the shallop appeared upriver. Moments later William Harwood stepped ashore, the gold threads in his brown velvet breeches winking brightly in the sunshine. He was a portly man who looked about him imperiously, as though expecting the gathered throng to fall to their knees before him. But the people were as excited at the sight of the crates of chickens, the four goats, and the kegs of meal and ale waiting to be unloaded, as they were at the sight of their leader.

Richard Kean stepped ashore behind the newcomer and raised a hand. The crowd fell silent.

Master Harwood cleared his throat. "I bring greetings from the adventurers of Martin's Hundred to the colonists who are working to create a civilization in the wilderness," he announced in a squeak.

Anne appeared beside Sarah, but the two did not dare look at each other for fear of squealing with laughter, for the man's high-pitched voice countered his sturdy appearance, and his habit of spraying spittle as he spoke made listening to him most amusing.

"Together we will build a fine plantation and make Virginia a rich, prosperous land," Harwood continued. "It will be my pleasure to direct you in that pursuit and to tell you that from now on, this settlement, the heart of Martin's Hundred, will be known as Wolstenholme Towne in honor of our chief supporter in London." He removed a handkerchief from beneath his starched cuff and dabbed his brow and mouth.

"He should wipe off those standing near him," Sarah whispered to Anne, "for no doubt they are well-sprayed."

With a wave, Harwood started along the track to the fort.

"Wolstenholme Towne?" said Anne. "My tongue stumbles over that name."

"Aye," agreed Margaret. "Instead of Master Harwood, I wish the lieutenant had found two milk cows on the *Bonaventure*."

The complaining talk at dinner that evening showed Margaret was not the only one who would have preferred a cow to William Harwood.

"He's not satisfied with anything we've done," groused Walter, jamming tobacco into his pipe. "Insists we should have more houses built and the church completed. We must begin immediately to repair the thatched roof on the fort dwelling where he is to live— and what he says about our crops I can't repeat before maidenly ears."

"But we had a hailstorm only yesterday," protested John. "Doesn't Mister Harwood realize we're lucky to have any crops at all? If the hailstones had been the size of my fist, as they sometimes are, every plant would be as flat as a squished chinch bug."

"We told him that," sighed Cisly, rubbing his chin. "Yet he seemed more concerned about the lost profits to the investors in London than about whether or not we starve come winter."

Anne rested her hand on Cisly's arm. "Did you tell him we spend all our days growing gardens and tobacco and have no time for building churches and houses?"

"It would have done no good," said Walter. "He'll have to see for himself."

"He has called for a church service next Sunday," added Cisly.

Margaret rubbed a hand wearily over her face. "We *have* neglected our worship. Yet we do our best, saying our daily prayers over meals and at bedtime. What more could Harwood expect, especially as Martin's Hundred has no regular minister?"

Hannah snorted. "Now, just as harvest is going *well,* we must spend precious time with our hands *clasped* together instead of stripping leaves."

The topmost leaves of the tobacco plants had that week rolled over to touch the ground, as though begging them to pull the ripe, yellow-spotted leaves from the plants. Even Sarah, who was not required to do fieldwork, had been helping to string the leaves on lines, hurrying while there was still hot weather to cure them to a bright color.

"Perhaps a day of worship will inspire us and make the work go faster," said Anne hopefully.

This time both Hannah and Margaret snorted.

"Harwood is very concerned about the natives," Cisly said. He looked at John. "Do you think the Indians will remain at peace?"

John nodded. "I do, though it will be no thanks to that strutting dandiprat Richard Kean. The way he drills us constantly and goes about dressed in his armor! He gives the impression he trusts the Indians not one whit!"

"He has a great responsibility," Margaret protested quietly. "He acts as he sees fit for the safety of the settlement. And he no longer wears a full suit of armor when he goes about his duties, none at all some of the time."

Walter leaned forward and emptied his pipe into the fireplace, the tap-tap-tap of clay on stone filling the silence between words. "Besides," he chided, "some people tend to be too trusting. Some go about with the natives, learning their ways—even learning to hunt with a bow and arrow, and dressing as a native."

Even in the dusk, Sarah could see John's color rise. "Our quarry strolls away while we fit the fuse of an unwieldy musket," he snapped. "A quick, silent bow is better!"

His tone, and the memory of the way John looked when she'd met him in the forest, made Sarah realize Walter had been speaking of John.

"No need to get into a *froth*," said Hannah, waving her arms in the air. "It may be John'll be proved *right* in the end."

"Indeed, I shall," John replied, kicking the heel of his boot against the stool leg. "People fear and distrust the natives because they don't know them; they don't make an attempt to understand and respect their ways, their thoughts."

The *hup-hup, oho-oho* of a horned owl drifted through the open door. "Some folk think the horned owl is *Indians* calling to each other in the *night*," Hannah said then.

"Are they correct?" Anne asked, slipping her hand into Cisly's.

John shrugged. "Perhaps—if the Indians were planning a surprise attack on their enemy." Again the owl hooted. "That call comes from a feathered creature though."

"Then it could be an Injun," piped Twig, "for they wear a great many feathers on 'em."

The others broke into laughter. "You have me there," John agreed. "They do indeed."

∞∞∞
Chapter 17

Autumn, the season the Indians called *cohonk,* had come. The heat of summer had fled, taking with it the biting gnats and flies, and bringing after it a soothing November sun and a sapphire sky often filled with the thunderous beating of wings, the honk of the wild goose, the cry of the swan and the mallard.

Sarah was so busy helping to gather the wild harvest—grapes, onions, nuts, berries—she tutored only three mornings a week. Walter built a turkey pen in the forest, and in one week captured nearly fifty of the birds, which he promptly beheaded. Sarah sneezed feathers for days as she helped pluck and clean them. Now she was helping to salt and smoke the carcasses for winter.

"If we had more salt, we could dry more game," grumped Margaret.

"Master Boys says a Lieutenant Craddock is to fix up the saltworks on Smith's Island come *spring*," said Hannah, who was also helping.

Margaret threw another dry corncob onto the smoking fire, then added another turkey to those already hanging from the strong pole above it. "Good. Perhaps next year we'll have enough salt." She straightened, and rubbed the small of her back, looking around at the trees decked with a joyous riot of russet, red, and gold. "At least this fine autumn weather has turned our tobacco harvest a mellow golden-brown. Soon it'll be time to carry it upriver to Jamestown."

If only I could go upriver with the tobacco, thought Sarah, rubbing her smoke-stung eyes. *If only I could sail all the way to England with it.* She sighed, thinking of the few baskets of soap ashes she had accumulated. At this rate it would be four years before she could go home to England. And tomorrow she would again have no time to make ashes. In the morning she had to help Margaret make candles from the grayish bayberries they had collected near Mulberry Island. Later, she and Twig were to gather sassafras bark for Margaret's medicine supply and crab apples for storing.

At midafternoon the next day Twig and Sarah crackled and crunched their way though the leaves that lay ankle deep on the forest floor. A wild wind in the night had torn most of the leaves from the trees. Now a wispy ray of sunshine glanced off the few tenacious ones still fluttering restlessly, like tattered hands waving them on their way.

They kept the river on their left, picking their way across trickling streams and around a marsh. Sarah marveled at how familiar the Virginia forest now seemed, no longer the frightening place it had been the first time she had traveled through it five months before.

Soon they came to a creek wider than the others.

"Must we cross this creek also?" Twig complained, scuffling his feet through the leaves and leaving a ruffled trail behind him.

"Not this one," Sarah replied. "Margaret told me the best crab apples are on this side." She stopped and sat on a newly fallen tree to catch her breath. Twig plunked his skinny frame down beside her.

"I wonder why no one's built a house 'ere?" he asked. "It's a fine, clear spot for 'un. On a creek and close to the river."

Sarah looked around. "As usual, there is certainly enough wood to build a house."

"Aye," agreed Twig, "but look there at those patches of clear ground. A fella could plant right away, without clearin' the cursed trees."

He was right, Sarah saw. It was perfect—for someone wanting land in Virginia. Her unclaimed headright flashed into her thoughts, then she shook her head.

"Come on," she told Twig, standing and straightening her bodice. "We better get busy. I want to get back before sunset. You gather apples, I'll cut bark."

After a while they rested, and Sarah mixed some *nocake*.

"Can we go home now?" asked Twig, licking the last of the sweet mixture of water and parched, powdered corn from his palm.

Sarah looked at their half-full baskets and shook her head. "Margaret will have our skins if we don't fill the baskets," she said.

Sarah was not skillful at cutting bark, and Twig spent more time pitching crab apples at targets than picking them, so the sun was setting when they finally filled their baskets.

Twig kept close to Sarah as they started through the darkening woods, Twig carrying the fruit, Sarah the bark. A breeze from the northwest crept under her shawl, making her skin prickle, though she wasn't cold. It's the same forest we walked through in the sunlight, Sarah told herself. But the trees felt closer, and the fluttering leaves seemed to reach toward them, instead of waving them on.

"I hope we have fine weather for the pig slaughter next week," Sarah said, hoping her voice would chase away the dread rising in her chest, as the forest grew darker still.

Twig replied with a timid squeak.

He runs about the woods acting brave in the daytime and teasing me about being afraid, Sarah thought, *but at night Twig is no braver than I.* She felt his small hand slip into hers, remembered he was only a child, and gave his hand a squeeze, which made her feel better as well.

Then a branch snapped to one side, and they froze. It was silent, and they moved on. But as soon as they began to walk, they heard the crackle of leaves, the padding of feet.

Twig pressed closer to her side. "It's only the swine," Sarah whispered, though she knew it wasn't true, for she heard no familiar grunting and woofing.

They stopped again, and Sarah freed her hand from Twig's and felt in the basket for the stripping knife Margaret had given her. Then she remembered she had set it down under the last tree and forgotten to pick it up again.

The stalker was as silent as they. Then came again a rustle of dry leaves, nearer than before. Sarah grabbed Twig's hand. "Run!" she whispered, and through the trees they raced, branches whipping their faces and roots snapping at their flying feet, fruit and bark bouncing out of the baskets.

In minutes, the smell of smoke from the settlement drifted through the barren trees. Breathless, they stumbled out of the woods into a field where brittle cornstalks rustled. When they reached the far end of the field they stopped, listening. The night was silent.

"I 'spect 'twas a panther," panted Twig, when their

terror and breathing had eased and they were cutting across the muddy track leading to the river.

At that moment a panther did scream from the woods behind them, and they shivered. As they reached the edge of the gully that led to the Davidsons', Sarah stopped and looked back toward the forest. The rising moon silvered the dried cornstalks—and the figure of an Indian standing motionless at the edge of the field.

"We were about to call out a search party," scolded Margaret moments later, as she dished out boiled beans, peas, corn, and pumpkin. "Well, at least you got the crab apples and bark and seem none the worse for your late arrival, though I was hoping you'd fill the baskets."

Twig looked sideways at Sarah, his eyebrows nearly shooting up beneath his thatch of hair, as though to say it was lucky the entire harvest was not strewn among the leaves somewhere in the dark forest. "We were chased by a panther," he announced as he took his bowl, then went on to tell of the padding feet and their race through the trees.

Sarah confessed to the loss of the knife, which made Walter groan and Margaret draw her lip into the hole made by her missing front teeth. Sarah promised to go back for the knife. She didn't mention the Indian. Even later, after she climbed the ladder to her sleeping pallet and settled on the corn-shuck mattress across the room from a sleeping Twig, it was not the Indian she remembered. Nor was it the padding of feet in the dark and their wild race through the trees. She remembered only the touch of Twig's small hand clutching hers.

CRCRCD

Chapter 18

With a grunt and a snuffle and a woof, the boar lumbered out of the woods, snouting along the trail of corn Margaret had scattered on the ground. The ponderous beast had spent the summer eating tuckahoe roots, the autumn eating acorns and nuts, and was now as heavy as two stout men.

At the sight of Walter and John, the gluttonous swine scarcely hesitated, and soon came to a halt inside the temporary pen Walter had built, drawn by the large pile of corn Margaret had poured there. Quickly Walter raised the ax and brought the poll down on the boar's head. Stunned, the animal slumped silently to the ground. John drew his knife and slit the swine's throat, and Twig came running with a kettle to catch the blood.

Sarah looked on horrorstruck, for she had never seen an animal slaughtered. The sound of the ax thunking against the creature's skull, the sight of John's knife opening its throat, the sticky-sweet smell of the blood made her breakfast rise in the back of her throat. She feared she might be ill. Then Margaret called her to help lift the kettle of boiling water from the fire, and she turned gratefully away. The slaughter wouldn't halt for her squeamishness. The bristles had to be scraped, the boar hung and gutted, the small intestines emptied and scraped clean, the meat salted and smoked. Later, Margaret and Sarah would make the fat into lard, the blood into pudding, the lean into sausage to stuff the intestines.

Moments later, Isaac Dolphenby, the settlement's only black-skinned servant, arrived to help heft the animal into the monstrous kettle, where the hot water would loosen the bristles.

"Take care, Twig," said John, as the men strained to lift the animal over the side of the kettle. Eager to prove himself, Twig, spattered with the animal's blood, had squirmed among the men and was pushing mightily.

Walter had just ordered him away, when Twig's arm caught beneath the boar's back. As the pig slid into the kettle, a shriek rent the crisp air. Twig's arm plunged elbow-deep into the scalding water.

For a moment everyone froze. Only the boar moved, settling with a quiet whoosh underneath the boiling water. Then John snatched the screeching Twig up in his arms and ran with him to the house, Margaret close behind. Sarah stood in a daze until Walter shouted, "Sarah! Go! Margaret will need you," and she stumbled after the sound of Twig's piercing screams.

John laid Twig on Margaret's bed, then returned to the slaughter. Twig no longer screamed, but he whimpered, and his thin body quivered as Sarah held his small head against her pounding breast and Margaret peeled the cloth of his sleeve off the blistering skin.

Recalling the pain from the small burns she had gotten from her fires, Sarah could imagine how Twig hurt.

"Tobacco," Margaret ordered, with a jerk of her head toward the ladder. "Fetch some leaves from my medicine supply."

Sarah was soon clambering back down the ladder on quivering legs, her arms full of tobacco leaves. Margaret made a healing poultice, which she wrapped about Twig's scalded arm and bound with clean linen.

"If this doesn't help, I'll try a poultice of mint. And we have the sassafras you gathered last week. I'll make an infusion for him to drink."

At last Margaret returned to the slaughter, leaving Sarah to sit with Twig, who finally slept.

Hours later, Margaret came into the house with a fresh joint of meat, which she strung in front of the fire on a strong, hempen string. Sarah still sat beside Twig, holding his good hand and thinking how the sleeping boy had squirmed his way into her heart, thinking, when she returned to England, how hard it would be to leave him.

Luckily, Twig did not get a fever in the days that followed, though the skin of his arm withered and fell away, taking small pieces of flesh with it. But after weeks of fresh dressings and poultices, scars and bright new skin began to form, and he was eager to make a pest of himself once again.

Visitors came often in the days Twig lay in bed: Anne and Cisly, John and Hannah, even Richard, though he seemed to appear most often when Anne was visiting. Sarah loved Anne's visits the most, but she also enjoyed it when Hannah arrived.

"You'll not be picking any more *pockets,* I reckon," Hannah teased Twig, for he had made no effort to hide his past. "That is your favored hand you near *ruined,* is it not?"

Twig grinned at her. "Me other hand is near as sly at filtchin'," he said, causing Hannah to twitch a hank of his unruly hair.

Though Richard paid scant attention to Twig, asking only after his health, John came bearing gifts: a musket carved from alder, a sling, an undersized bow and arrows, a whistle of willow whose sound was so piercing that Margaret forbade Twig to blow it in the house.

Richard was present when John gave Twig the bow. "It's bad enough to take heathen ways upon yourself," he said, his brow a furrowed field of disapproval, "but must you teach them to the young as well?"

"Many Indian ways are wise ways." A muscle near the scar on John's right cheek twitched, and Sarah could sense anger in his voice, though he held it well. He was, after all, a servant, and couldn't voice his true thoughts.

"It's our duty to civilize the natives and convert them to Christianity," Richard snapped, "not to be seduced by their savage ways, as you seem to have been." He tugged at the hem of his doublet and sat straighter on his stool. "I believe our efforts are useless," he continued, his dark eyes narrowing, "unless we rid the tribes of their headmen." He raised his head and looked straight at John. "And even more useless as long as some of us admire the heathen ways."

The room was quiet for a heartbeat. Then John said, his soft voice a contrast to the harsh look in his eyes, "If to rid the tribes of their headmen means to kill them, that act would only make us more like the 'savages' and give us less hope for making them more like us." He, too, drew himself straighter on his stool. "If it's true, as my father used to quote, that a man reaps what he sows, then perhaps we should sow the seeds of understanding and friendship, not the seeds of hatred and distrust."

Hannah looked down at her roughened hands, no doubt worrying that John was at risk for speaking his mind. Walter cleared his throat and scraped his pipe into the fireplace. Margaret scurried about arranging trenchers and noggins, though these had been put carefully away hours before.

Well-spoken, Sarah thought, and she was surprised to

discover she agreed more with John than with Richard. Though she didn't feel completely at ease in the presence of an Indian, Sarah was slowly becoming accustomed to having them around the settlement. And just because they still made her uneasy didn't mean they should be murdered, as Richard seemed to suggest.

Richard's lips were drawn tight. "I fear you are mistaken," he said to John. "We will not be safe in Virginia until the last Indian lies dead with a musket ball through his heart. I pray you come to believe me before it is too late, and you, instead, lie dead." With that pronouncement, he rose to his feet and left the house.

Chapter 19

In December, a month in which snow sifted down to lie wet upon the ground for a few days before vanishing, the *Temperance* arrived in Jamestown bringing news that the *Mayflower* had landed many miles to the north at a place called Plymouth Rock.

In January 1621, the *Bona Nova* brought eighteen new settlers for Martin's Hundred. As they stepped onto the wharf, the wind blew in from the north, sharp and piercing, which meant, Walter said, a heavy frost that night. Sarah, who had come to watch the shallop being unloaded, wiggled her toes in the fur-lined shoes Rawhunt had given her, the ones he called *moccasins*, and pulled her cloak tightly about her shoulders.

Twig stood beside Sarah, his thin shoulders hunched under a tattered blanket against the damp cold. "More tools," he grumbled as the men began to unload the boats after the newcomers had been led away.

Sarah's stomach rumbled as broad-hoes, axes, shovels, gimlets for boring holes, frowes for splitting shingles, glass beads, muskets, swords, lead, and powder were carried off the shallop.

"No oatmeal," muttered Twig, flapping his scrawny arms to keep warm.

"Or wheat, butter, or cheese," said Sarah wistfully. "I suppose another long voyage, or a greedy captain who didn't want to buy his own provisions, meant the passengers ate all the food the Company was sending to *us*." She stamped her feet in the snow, as much in anger as to warm them. "What are these new people to eat? Our larders are nearly empty." She sighed. "Who would have dreamed that all the food we put by last summer wouldn't be enough, thanks to our growing numbers? If only the hunting would get better."

For weeks the men had been going out with their muskets, but with little success. Rawhunt and another Indian, Ipitaquod, had come to the Davidsons' a time or two bearing hare or squirrel, but these had scarcely begun to fill the settlers' hungry bellies. Sarah nearly laughed to think how frightened she'd been of the Indians when she first arrived. Now they were a welcome sight indeed. But the most welcome sight of all would be the misty coast of England upon her return, Sarah told herself, wondering, as she often did, if she should take Anne's advice to claim her land and plant tobacco to help earn her fare. Twig's voice echoed her thoughts of home.

"If we don't get somethin' to eat soon," he grouched quietly, "I'll wish I *had* gone back to London to filtch purses." His gray eyes loomed so large in his shrunken face they made Sarah's heart clench.

"There 'ee goes!" shouted Will later that week, and a club smashed down on the scurrying rat before it could escape the circle of people. Will tossed it onto the pile with the rest.

"We're too short of food to allow vermin to eat our corn," Harwood had announced a few days earlier. "They're destroying bushels every week. We'll have a rat killing."

Now the people of Martin's Hundred stood in a circle around the corn pile, sticks held ready, while the rain beat upon the thatch of the company storehouse.

Sarah stood near the door, a long branch in her hand, praying no rat scampered toward her. She recalled the rat that had snuffled around Aunt Mary's head the night she fell ill aboard the *Jonathan*, and her skin prickled at the memory. *If one of the creatures comes my way,* she thought, *I'll probably run shrieking from the storehouse and disgrace myself before my friends and neighbors.*

One-handed, so as not to jar his sore arm, Twig picked up a few more ears of corn and tossed them from the shrinking old pile onto the growing pile beside it. With a squeak, another rat, deprived of its cover under the cobs, streaked for safety. *Thunk!* It, too, was added to the vermin heap. The killing went on until all the ears had been pitched onto the new pile, and the potter William James was declared champion rat killer.

Everyone then relaxed on the barrels stacked about the store. Many looked like strangers with their gaunt faces and hollow, black-smudged eyes. Jacob and Rose, leaner than ever, had come. Sarah didn't know why, for it was some distance to their house, and they were not ones to search out fellowship and gaiety, though there was little enough of *that* in these hungry times, and a rat killing was not exactly a cheerful event.

"What do we do with the dead 'uns?" asked Jonas Turner, kicking at a rat with his boot.

"We burn them," said Richard, who had come to supervise the killing.

"A cursed shame that 'ud be," said Turner, grabbing a rat and hefting it by its tail. Blood dripped from the creature's mouth, and its rodent teeth glinted in the dim light. "These be right plump rats, thanks to our corn. Lots of tasty meat on 'em."

Bile rose in Sarah's throat. Aghast, she saw Twig, Rose, and a few others nodding.

"Ate 'em on the ship coming over," said Hugh Roberts. "Least those with money did. Went for sixteen shillings a piece. I recall one woman—expecting a baby she was—who paid twenty shillings for one scrawny one. She died anyways."

"They taste like squirrel or rabbit," said Turner.

"Aye, they're not bad at all," echoed Twig.

Walter stalked over to Twig and grabbed him by his scruff. "Hungry though we are," he said, "we'll not fall so low as to eat vermin. Now you get home before I take an inch off that scrawny hide of yours."

Twig scurried toward the door. As he passed Sarah, he rolled his eyes and licked his lips. *Even hunger doesn't dim his rascally nature,* she thought, almost giggling in spite of herself.

Everyone started to argue then, some wanting to eat the rats, some, such as John and Hannah, saying they'd die of hunger before the filthy meat ever touched their lips. Although Sarah's insides ached for food, she sided with the Clarks, though she knew how much Hannah, whose baby was due in May, needed nourishing food.

"Silence!" roared Richard at last. "The rats will be burned." He then ordered people to carry them outside, where a fire could be safely set.

Sarah refused to touch the repulsive pests, but many scuttled over to the heap to comply. A while later, when the rain-dampened blaze finally caught and the rats began to burn, the pile looked suspiciously smaller than it had earlier, inside the storehouse.

Jacob and Rose passed Sarah moments later, hurrying to cross the gully. Sarah thought Rose's cloak looked rather lumpy where it was pulled tightly about her body, and she shuddered, certain what Rose had hidden there and wondering if rat meat did taste like squirrel or rabbit.

That evening they ate a gruel made from dried peas and were forced to drink water, the ale having run dry a few days past. Thinking of the meal Rose and Jacob were sharing, Sarah nearly gagged, then downed the gruel and water more willingly. Yet she thought Twig had a hungry look of longing in his eye.

I won't survive four years in this land, Sarah told herself, as she had many times since the hunger began. *Perhaps Anne is right. If I file for my headright, come spring I could plant my own tobacco and earn more money for my fare home.*

She shook her head. Land was a tie to Virginia, and she wanted nothing to hold her there.

But it would be only a temporary tie, she told herself, *a tie easily severed.*

The work will be harder than any you have done before, a voice in her head warned.

No matter how hard the work, she answered back, *if it helps me leave this wretched land sooner, it will be worth it. So I will claim my headright.* Her decision made, Sarah plopped her spoon into her empty bowl and rose to clear the board.

Chapter 20

Sarah didn't claim her headright in February, because by then the people of Martin's Hundred were dying. Starvation and disease took its toll. Few people left their houses. One was Richard, who was in charge of burials; another was John, ordered by Richard to do the digging and to lay the dead in the bare, cold earth. With plague spreading, haste was necessary, so the bodies were wrapped only in linen, with no coffin to shelter them. They lost Ralph Chelsey and his wife Eliza, old Laurence Collier, and baby Frances Snow all on the same day.

How glad I'll be to smell the blossoms of spring and not the stench of death, Sarah thought.

By the middle of March the dying had ended. Once again the sky was black with birds, this time flying northward. The fish that wintered in salt water were entering the rivers, and the Indians brought herring, shad, rockfish, or trout nearly every day.

One day, when the air was adrift with springtime smells and her four pupils sent off, Sarah decided it was warm enough to do the washing. But the stream running past her maple was icy cold and froze her hands to the marrow. She pounded the wooden beetle on the clothing harder, and harder still, trying to beat some warmth back into her numb fingers. At last she rinsed the wash in the stream and hung it to dry on the bushes. She shook some life back into her hands, then climbed the maple and sat gazing upward to the blue sky, thinking she felt no older today, on March 22, her fifteenth birthday, than she had the day before.

Perhaps I'll visit Anne this afternoon and tell her it's my birthday, and then I will feel older, Sarah thought. *Or perhaps I'll feel older tomorrow, when I sail to Jamestown to sell my lumps of soap ashes and claim my headright.*

The following afternoon Edward Sharpless, the clerk of the court, exploded into nasal laughter, his nostrils flapping, one hand held against his thin chest. "A landholder! The lady wishes to be a landholder!" he chortled. "Indeed, this job is a revelation."

Sarah's color rose and her tongue swelled into uselessness.

"Is there any law stating the lady may not claim her headright?" asked Richard calmly.

During the voyage upriver, Sarah had sat, silent and alone, among her soap ashes. When they disembarked, Richard had said, much to her dismay, "You need a man to go with you to the clerk. Women, and especially young girls, can't be expected to handle matters concerning property." When Sarah had looked hopefully toward Master Jackson, Richard had added, "Master Jackson will be supervising the delivery of our goods to the store. I am the only one free to accompany you."

Now, for the first time ever, Sarah was glad of Richard's presence.

Sharpless seemed not to have heard Richard's question, and his laughter continued. Richard's left eyebrow twitched, a sign, Sarah knew, he was becoming annoyed at the man.

Perhaps claiming my land isn't a good idea, she thought. *Perhaps I should forget it.* She was about to suggest they leave when the door opened. Round John Pory entered. He was the secretary for the Council, who Sarah recalled had sampled all the beer at the governor's tea so many months before.

"What merriment!" he chuckled. "I cannot resist the sound of merriment, so I came to see what the fun is all about. Lieutenant Kean, is it not?" he asked, reaching out a hand to Richard, "and ... and ..." He hesitated, looking with a bright grin at Sarah, who immediately dropped her gaze to the man's mud-encrusted boots.

"Mistress Douglas," Richard said, nodding toward Sarah and extending his own hand.

"So tell me," Pory went on. "What is the cause of the jocularity?"

"We were explaining to the clerk that Mistress Douglas wishes to file for her headright," explained Richard. "The simpleton seems to find the thought amusing."

As Sharpless sputtered in rage at Richard's namecalling, John Pory looked at Sarah. He studied her for a time, then gave her a merry wink before turning to the clerk. "Now, Edward," he said, "what's all the pother?"

"I've never had a person of *her* sort file for a headright before," he muttered defensively.

"Of what sort might she be?" asked Pory.

"You know—a female," he spat.

Master Pory tapped his lips thoughtfully. "Is there any law forbidding such a person from claiming a headright?"

"A wife may not make a claim of her own," Sharpless ventured.

"Well, mistress." Master Pory turned to Sarah. "Are you someone's wife?"

Sarah shook her head no, feeling her breath come easier.

"Are you someone's servant?"

Again Sarah shook her head.

"Someone's widow?"

"No."

"Someone's intended?"

She denied it, blushing fiercely.

Pory waved his stocky arms in the clerk's face. "She belongs to no man. Therefore, the lady is free to make a claim on her headright if she can take the oath with a clear conscience.

"We usually conduct this sort of business when the Assembly is in session," he explained, after Sharpless had written down the required information. Giving her no time to protest or shrink away, Pory took Sarah by the arm and led her outside. "That is when we have most of the Council together." He peered into her face, nearly overwhelming Sarah with his foul breath. "You must swear the oath before the governor and Council that you paid your own fare to Virginia."

"I, indeed, paid my own fare," Sarah told him, pulling her elbow out of his grasp and stepping back.

"Then I shall do what I can to see you do not go home disappointed." Pory stood for a moment, rubbing his chin whiskers with a broad finger, then said, "I think I can corner Rolfe and Maycock. Those two, plus myself and the governor, should be enough to hear your oath. Meet me tomorrow, an hour after sunrise at the Governor's Mansion.

"I suppose the lieutenant will come, too?" he asked, his voice sorrowful.

Richard nodded. "In the absence of William Harwood, I feel it is my duty to help expedite this matter for Mistress Douglas, since she lives in my settlement and has no one to watch out for her. So, yes, I will come, too.''

"I was afraid of that," Pory said, smacking a pudgy fist into a pudgy palm, then whispering, "I had hoped to have you all to myself." With another wink he hurried off, taking no notice of Sarah's reddening cheeks or her wide eyes.

"You are free to bide at my house this night," he called over his shoulder to Richard. "Ask any person the way, or just follow the sound of the merrymaking."

When Pory had disappeared around a corner, Richard gave a slight shake of his head and turned to Sarah. "I'll see you to the home of the Pierces," he said.

Sarah stood chewing on her thumbnail as the four men huddled together, their voices a whisper she couldn't make out. Governor Yeardley, John Rolfe, Samuel Maycock, and John Pory had been waiting at the Governor's Mansion when Richard and Sarah arrived the next morning. At first it seemed Sarah would soon have her headright, but when she was about to take the oath, Edward Sharpless, there to issue her certificate, had leaned over to whisper in the governor's ear. Yeardley frowned, then turned to Sarah.

"Would you please tell us your age, Mistress Douglas," he said.

"Fifteen," Sarah replied in a timid voice.

Upon hearing her answer, all the men frowned except Edward Sharpless, who had an open grin on his narrow, pocked face.

Now the men were whispering together, and Sarah didn't know what the problem might be.

"There seems to be some question as to whether we can grant a headright to one so young," Governor

Yeardley said at last, settling himself in his green velvet chair.

Sarah's heart lurched. Her head swirled and her knees went limp. If she didn't get her headright, she would have no place to plant tobacco, and it would be years before she could return home to England. But she didn't dare tell that to the waiting men. Knowing she wanted the land only as a means to escape Virginia might not sit well with them. So, not knowing what to say, she stood silent and shaken, the men's gaze fixed upon her.

Then, as sometimes had happened on board the *Jonathan*, when it was darkest and Sarah had despaired of surviving the voyage, she felt her father at her shoulder, his thin body stooping over her, just as he once did while she recited Greek or Latin, while she did her numbers or practiced the harpsichord. "If thou faint in the day of adversity, thy strength is small," his voice echoed deep in Sarah's memory. Proverbs. Her father's favorite, perhaps because he wasn't strong himself and hoped to instill in her what he lacked.

A cold calm enfolded Sarah. Her thoughts settled, and a courage she had never known flowed through her. "It's true I've seen few years," she said quietly, her eyes staring at the wall behind the governor. "But I make my own way in the world. I'm servant, ward, wife to no one. I'm indebted to neither man nor Company, having paid my own fare to Virginia and having survived the voyage, which my only relative did not." With difficulty, Sarah stopped her hand from brushing away a tear that was threatening to spill from her eye and, instead, took a loud gulp of air. "I hope you'll take it upon yourselves to grant me my headright in spite of my youth," she continued, her voice growing stronger, "for it is my dream. It was likely a dream that brought each of you to this land. Pray, sirs, do not deny me mine." She took another gulp of air, hoping

Richard had not heard of her wish to go home to England. A word from him about her true dream would ruin everything.

The men began to mutter together again, and the tone did not sound encouraging. Sarah braced herself for disappointment.

"I also wish to speak," Richard interrupted then, causing Sarah's heart to thud so loudly she was certain everyone could hear.

The governor nodded.

"I have been aware of Mistress Douglas since her departure from England," he said. "Having spent a good portion of my life in the king's service, living the life of a soldier in foreign countries, I know how difficult it is to be alone in the world. Yet Mistress Douglas has borne that burden with a courage even I admire." Richard stopped to clear his throat, but did not look toward Sarah, who was staring in amazement at the man she thought so cold and unfeeling. "Should more such as her choose to come to Virginia," he continued, "this will be a land of great prosperity, for she is a willing worker who goes far beyond the task demanded of her. She tutors the indentured children. She labors to make soap ashes—as the Company has requested. Gentlemen, she even labors in the fields."

At his last words the men gasped.

"Fieldwork!" said John Pory, shaking his head. "Not even indentured women do fieldwork. Only the most beastly among them. It seems Mistress Douglas is, indeed, contributing more than her share to the betterment of Virginia."

Again the men went into a huddle. Edward Sharpless watched with a frown and chewed on his lower lip. Sarah gathered what courage she had left and gave Richard a grateful smile, thinking that help comes from the most unlikely places, and wondering what Richard would think if he knew his words were helping her to leave the very land he thought she cared for?

"Place your hand upon the Bible," said Governor Yeardley, turning at last to Sarah. "You may take the oath and claim your headright."

A short time later, a breathless Sarah held in her hand the certificate that confirmed she was entitled to one hundred acres of land. She thought how pleased her mother would have been to know the family would once again be landowners. *But this is Virginia, not England,* she reminded herself. *Have I done the right thing? Will this land be the magic sail that carries me home, or that giant anchor I saw binding me to the New World?*

Chapter 21

Cattapeuk, the season of spring blossoms, had begun. Rain fell often, softening the ground for the tobacco Sarah was transplanting on her land. Her land. Sarah still felt shivery with hope when she said those words.

"Will you come to live here then?" Twig had asked, a tiny catch in his voice, when, after much searching, Sarah had decided he was right about the spot where they had gathered bark and crab apples and had chosen it for her own.

"Not for a long while yet." She had no intention of telling Twig she would never live on the land, that it was simply a means to escape from Virginia. Yet Sarah couldn't help feeling a small twitch of pride as she looked at the tall trees, the gushing creek, the small clearing that would be perfect for a house. She gave her head a quick shake to clear away such silly thoughts.

"Virginia has no surveyor to locate the grant and mark the boundaries," Sarah explained to Twig, "so I have no title, and it's not yet rightfully mine. I wouldn't feel free to build a house here until it was. But I'll plant on it."

Twig gave a gusty sigh of relief. "Then perhaps

you'll not leave us till I am free and can come with you," he ventured, the worry gone from his voice.

"Perhaps not," Sarah agreed, though she knew she would be back in England long before Twig was twenty years old.

All Sarah's free time since she had claimed her land had been spent getting it ready to plant. She had borrowed a hoe from the storehouse, and Walter had showed her how to chop the earth in the clearest spaces into fine, smooth soil. Next, following Walter's instructions, she had hilled the earth, every four-and-a-half feet drawing it into a round, knee-high mound about her leg. After, she carefully pulled her leg free, leaving a hole where her leg had been. Twenty times she had done this, leaving twenty hills with twenty holes.

Now it was time to place the young plants in the holes. Already Twig was walking among the hills, dropping a plant beside each one.

Twenty hills. Twenty plants. It was all she could afford with the money she had earned from her soap ashes. Sarah shrugged, looking at the thick callouses on her palms and remembering how her back had ached, how the sweat had dripped, when she was working the soil. Even if she had money for more plants, she couldn't have hoed more hills before planting time. It was the hardest work she had ever done in her life. Only knowing it would take her home had kept her at it.

"I think I'll hoe one new hill each day after these are planted," she shouted to Twig, as she bent to gently pat the soil around the roots of the first plant. "That way, when I can buy more plants, the hills will be ready, and the work won't seem so hard if I do a little bit at a time."

"Growin' 'bacca is hateful hard work even a bit at a time," groused Twig, tossing down his empty basket. "I just finished the easiest part." He rubbed his forearm. Though the burns had healed well, there was scarring and stiffness, and he tended to favor the arm at times.

"It is hard work, but it doesn't seem so bad when you're doing it for yourself. You'll learn that someday when you have land of your own."

"If I ever get land of me own, I for sure won't plant 'bacca. Next Walter says it's weedin', weedin', weedin', and after that toppin'. You'll be glad ya planted only a few of the cursed things." Twig pulled an impish face at her. "I 'spect I'll be glad, too."

Sarah grinned at him, noting how he had shot up over the past few months, but how he stayed true to his name, his bony arms and legs poking out in all directions. "Bend a knee," she ordered, "before the roots shrivel and all my hard work is wasted."

The two had planted over half the hills when Rawhunt appeared, standing before Sarah, a small rug made of beaver skins over his arm. "To trade," he said.

Sarah smiled to herself as she reached out to touch the fur. Scarcely a year ago she had seen her first native Virginian and was certain they would forever strike terror into her heart. John was right—fear and distrust did come from not knowing a person.

"It would make a perfect gift for Hannah's infant," she told Twig, who had come near to admire the rug. "She should birth it in a few weeks. But I have nothing to trade."

"Your pin." Twig pointed at the brooch Sarah had that morning stuck onto the collar of her gown. It had belonged to Aunt Mary, and Sarah had worn it in honor of the day she first planted tobacco on her own land, knowing Aunt Mary would be proud.

"I'd forgotten it." Sarah opened the clasp and held the brooch in her palm. It was not one of her favorites. Still, it would be hard to part with, because it had been her aunt's favorite. Finally Sarah shrugged. A warm cover for a new baby was more important than a pretty bauble. She held it out to Rawhunt. "I will trade."

The Indian shook his head. Pointing to where Walter's musket leaned against a nearby log, he said, "Want gun. You take beaver, I take gun."

After a bear with cubs had attacked Humphrey Walden not far from the settlement, Walter had taught Sarah how to use the musket and insisted she take it with her whenever she worked on her land.

It was Sarah's turn to shake her head. "I can't trade you the gun. It's not my gun to trade. This is all I have." She waggled the pin so the purple stone caught the light.

At last Rawhunt plucked it from her, turning it one way then another, watching the glint and flash of the stone and metal. "Good." He handed Sarah the fur and headed inland. "Next time I trade with Walter. Then I get gun."

As Rawhunt disappeared, John came panting up, his face scarlet. "It's time," he gasped. "Hannah's pains have started. Margaret needs you."

Sarah covered her mouth with a dirt-grimed hand. "But it's too soon, and I know nothing about birthing babies. Get Mistress Boys."

"She faints if someone cuts a finger." John waved her to come.

Sarah turned to Twig. "Will you finish the last plants for me? There are fewer than ten left. I'll leave you Walter's musket."

Twig puckered his mouth, but nodded, and Sarah hurried after John, the beaver rug in her arms. When they were nearly out of hearing, Twig shouted after them. To Sarah, it sounded like, "Don't let Rose near the wee 'un."

* * *

John and Sarah found Hannah busy by the fireplace, calmly stirring a mess of vegetables and hanging tiny garments before the fire to warm.

"Why aren't you in bed?" John asked in alarm.

Hannah grinned. "I *told* you there was no *hurry*."

Margaret glanced up from where she squatted, sorting through her medicine basket. "A first child comes slowly. And Hannah insisted there be enough food for you to eat tonight."

"I am *glad* you have come, Sarah," Hannah said then. "Ever since the hungry time, I've been *worrying* about this babe, so I shall welcome another *friendly* face beside me." She poured some hot water for Sarah to wash in, then waved her wooden spoon at John. "You go and chop wood or finish that *stool* you started last week."

John went, looking as though he had been scolded.

The afternoon shadows were stretched thin when Hannah's pains began in earnest. Sarah and Margaret helped her into her nightgown and made her as comfortable as possible on the bed. Then Sarah prepared a trencher of food for John, who sat on the doorstep whittling on a stool leg that was becoming much too thin.

By sunset Sarah had chewed off four fingernails, and Hannah was becoming exhausted. Sarah dozed off and on through the night, while the child refused to come, but Margaret stayed watchful. As the dark began to retreat before the dawn, she went at last to her basket. "Hannah is becoming too wearied."

From the basket Margaret drew a pouch. It was filled with powder she had dried from the jelly found in the head of a drum fish. Quickly she made some powder into a broth, which she held to Hannah's lips. "Drink. This will hurry the little one up."

When the baby came, Sarah closed her eyes, shutting out everything except Hannah's groans, her gasping breaths. She would have been happy to keep them closed, except that after Hannah had lapsed into silence, Margaret snapped, "Look alive, girl! I need some help here."

Sarah opened her eyes to see Margaret holding a wrinkled, blood-smeared mite of a person. Before Sarah could comment, Margaret thrust the baby into Sarah's hands, shook her head, then, to Sarah's puzzlement, silently placed a stained finger to her lips.

It was then Sarah noticed the baby wasn't moving, that it had uttered no cry, that it seemed to be growing colder even as she held it. She watched numbly as Margaret felt the cord that still attached the baby to Hannah, shook her head again, shrugged, then quickly tied two narrow strips of linen about the cord, took up a sharp knife, and cut between the ties.

Turning to Sarah, she took the baby from her and ordered, "Hand me some of those soft cloths we warmed." Then, sitting on a stool near the fire, she spread the cloths on her lap, laid the baby on the cloths and, with a shake of her head, as though she knew it were hopeless, began rubbing the baby with her hands. Rubbing, rubbing, rubbing.

Time seemed to stop for Sarah then. She was aware of the snap of the fire, of Hannah's raspy breaths, of the sun starting to pry its way into the room, of an odor that reminded her of the pig slaughter. But she seemed to be looking down on the scene from a point high and far away.

At last Margaret's hands slowed, then stopped. When Hannah groaned, Margaret motioned Sarah to come and take the baby. Sarah moved toward her, feeling as though she were floating, the way she sometimes floated in her dreams. But when she felt the baby in her arms again, she was back in the real world, and time was moving.

The baby was a boy, she noticed. John would have loved a son. She thought of John sitting anxiously on the doorstep and wondered if he had whittled away the entire stool leg.

Margaret's voice broke into her thoughts. "Wrap the babe and put him in the cradle. Then bring me the rest of the cloths. Hannah won't stop bleeding."

For the next hour the women ignored the occasional knock at the door, the occasional muffled question, as Margaret turned from Hannah to her basket and back to Hannah, searching for the one magic potion that would staunch the woman's bleeding.

"She's so white," Sarah whispered, wiping Hannah's face with a cool cloth, remembering how common she had thought Hannah when she had first met her and heard her swooping voice, seen her coarsened hands, the hairs sprouting on her upper lip.

"Baby," Hannah whispered in a voice Sarah could scarcely hear. Once again Margaret shook her head.

"A baby boy," Sarah told her.

"Benjamin," sighed Hannah, the name using nearly all the strength she had left.

"Benjamin Clark. That's a lovely name." Sarah brushed Hannah's hair back from her forehead and swallowed a gulp of tears.

"Call John in," Margaret whispered.

"But what about . . ." Sarah looked toward the still bundle lying under the beaver rug in the cradle, then back to Hannah.

"Call him." Then, nodding toward Hannah, Margaret silently mouthed the words, "She's dying."

Sarah couldn't bring herself to go back into the cabin with John. Instead, she sat on the stool he had left. Under her feet was a pile of shavings. The sweet smell of the wood drifted up, and she took deep breaths to try and still the shudders sweeping over her.

Moments later, John's groan told Sarah that Hannah was dead, and Sarah became aware that her clenched fists were full of crumpled shavings. John's footsteps crossed to the cradle. Sarah pictured him folding back the fur rug to look at his son. She kicked at the pile of shavings, then ran toward the gully and her maple.

A warm rain was falling the next day as they buried Hannah and Benjamin, the gabled lid of the single coffin the last thing poking through the dirt that spattered down upon it. As the last shovelful covered even that, John turned away, his face full of anguish, and Sarah saw reflected there the pain she had felt when she lost her mother, her father, her aunt. At that moment John's pain became her pain, and she wished she were bold enough to reach out and hold him while they wept.

∽∽∽
Chapter 22

It was May 1621. Sarah had lived in Virginia for a year, yet her thoughts were often of England. She missed the feel of cobblestones beneath her feet and the cry of the mongers selling their wares: fresh-baked loaves, bright red roses decked with dew, meat pasties, colorful ribbons, dainty gloves.

But she also remembered the bitter taste of the London air, at times so thick with soot and smoke she could scarcely draw a breath. She recalled the filthy street urchins scurrying and darting among the carriages, and shook her head at the thought that Twig had been one. Remembering the ear-thrumming throngs of people swarming through the streets filled her with both joyful anticipation and trepidation. How would it feel to live again among so many after living among so few? For even though more than one thousand new colonists had arrived in Virginia in the last year, that many had also died, and in all of Virginia the population still numbered just over eight hundred.

The number of Sarah's pupils had grown to six; two were the children of settlers. One day she took them outside under her maple tree to hear them recite from Ovid.

"Forsan et haec olim meminisse iuvabit," read Will in a tentative voice.

"Translate please, Mottrom," Sarah ordered.

"Perhaps some day it will be ... will be ... pleasant to ... to remember even this," the boy finished, his voice prideful.

"Excellent!" Sarah said, just as Twig sniggered loudly.

"What do you find so amusing?" Sarah's look was stern.

"I doubt I shall ever find it pleasant to remember lessons."

Sarah was about to deliver a lecture on the benefits of an education, when a loud screeching filled the air. Ordering the children to stay where they were, she ran to the other side of the house, toward the noise.

Margaret, tucking up a few strands of loose hair, trotted out of the palisade gate to join her, as Jacob Howe pranced out of the trees on the far side of the field, his thin arms waving about his tufted head, his legs flailing out on both sides. Then the usually silent man whooped like an Indian. He was still for a moment, his head high and pivoting from side to side. Then he started once again to leap about.

As Jacob drew nearer, squeals and chortles burst from his lips, which were drawn back from his teeth in an oafish leer. His eyes seemed immense in his head, and now and then rolled backward into his skull.

"Take care, Sarah," warned Margaret.

Sarah thought uneasily of the children seated under the maple tree. Running back to them, she dismissed the class and ordered them home.

"Blow me!" said Twig, when he followed Sarah back to Margaret and saw Jacob prancing about. "The man is tainted in the 'ead."

Walter had heard the noise and came running from

the field, where he was hoeing tobacco with Isaac Dolphenby. They circled Jacob, their hoes ready should he attack them.

But it was soon clear that Jacob was a happy fool, not a dangerous one. He continued to gambol about until finally he sank to the ground, exhausted by his antics.

Twig moved behind Sarah as Rose stepped out of the woods. No doubt she had been lurking there, watching and waiting to see what would become of her demented husband. Walking over to where the flush-faced Jacob sat, she prodded him with her bare foot. He silently toppled sideways. Then, with a quiet giggle, he fell asleep.

"Merriest he's been since we wed," Rose commented dryly.

"Whatever made him so?" Margaret bent down to peer into Jacob's face. "He wasn't bitten by a wild animal, was he?"

"Don't think so," Rose answered. "It started yesterday, it did, soon after the evening meal. He was in a fine, feverish froth all night, I tell you."

"You mean he has been like this all night?" asked Walter.

"That's what I said," snapped Rose, briefly reminding Sarah of the Rose she had known on the voyage. But then she hung her head and reverted to the new, timid Rose.

"What did you feed him for the evening meal?" Margaret's tone was such that not even the old Rose could refuse to answer.

"Fish, corn cakes, some greens I picked."

"What did the greens look like?"

Rose described the young shoots she had boiled and fed to Jacob.

"Jamestown weed," said Margaret then, making a

sucking noise through the space in her teeth. "It turns those who eat it into fools for a time. You'll not be picking it again, I'll wager."

"Indeed not," said Rose, her tone submissive.

Walter and Isaac hefted Jacob up and carried him home. Rose followed behind, her shoulders slumped, her fingers plucking at the cloth of her skirt.

"Visited Hannah at the birthin', didn't she," muttered Twig at Sarah's elbow, as the foursome disappeared.

"No, she did not. Why ever would you say that? And what would it matter anyway?"

Twig's only answer was a shrug.

For three more days Jacob would appear suddenly, to leap and somersault through the fields, to burst forth with loud, raucous noises.

"He should be purged to rid him of the black and yellow bile that is making him act like this," muttered Harwood in his moist, squeaky voice on the evening of the first day, when he unexpectedly dropped by for a visit and Jacob came whooping past the palisade.

"It won't be me who gives him the fever root or administers a clyster," Margaret told the head of the hundred.

"Then perhaps he should be confined to the storehouse."

Margaret shook her head. "He does no harm."

"He's most jolly to watch," added Twig.

So Harwood assigned Twig the job of following Jacob about to see he did not get lost in the forest or come to harm, and the man was allowed to wander at will.

On the third day the spell of the weed wore off. Jacob went stomping home, his head drawn down between his shoulders like a turtle pulling into its shell, his eyes glinting angrily.

"I hope Rose doesn't feed Jacob the Jamestown weed again," Sarah told Twig, as they watched him go.

"No doubt she was tryin' to poison 'im. I fancy she is right sorry her plan didn't work. P'hraps she'll put a moccasin snake in 'is boot next time."

Sarah shook her head, her loose curls bobbing around her cheeks. "Watching Jacob cavort turned you into a joker. Jacob doesn't seem the kindest husband, but I can't imagine even Rose punishing him in such a vile way. Poison him, indeed!"

"Ya do not know 'er," Twig said quietly. "And ya did not see Rose prancin' about as a fool, did ya?"

At first Sarah did not take his meaning. Later, in bed, while the odors of bayberry, sassafras, onions, parsley, and sorrel—hung in the loft to dry—drifted around her, she thought about what Twig had said. Only then did she understand. If Rose had not been trying to do something to Jacob, why hadn't she eaten any of the weed herself?

Toward morning, Twig's cries awakened Sarah. "Do not hurt it! Do not hurt it!" he whimpered. "It is such a wee thing." He began to sob.

Sarah rolled off the wooden bed Walter had made her, crept over to where Twig lay, and jostled his shoulder. "Wake up. Wake up. You're having a nightmare." Finally Sarah could see Twig's eyes gleaming round and fearful in the dusky light. "It was about Rose, wasn't it? You know something about her."

Twig nodded. "I know somethin' fearful bad 'bout 'er."

"Tell me. It will be our secret." The softness of Sarah's voice belied the pounding of her heart. Her palms grew damp.

Twig's old-man eyes peered at Sarah. "Promise ya'll keep it a secret?"

130

"I promise."

Twig shivered, and only after more coaxing did he tell. "She did somethin' most cruel," he whispered, gulping back tears. "Somethin' most cruel. Rose killed 'er own baby. She killed 'er baby."

Sarah's gasp filled the early-morning quiet. It was a while before her breath came back and her stomach stopped churning. She wiped her sweating hands on her nightgown. "Tell me, Twig. Everything."

The boy, Sarah learned, had known Rose in London when they were both living on the streets. Rose supported herself in much the same way as Twig and his friends—by picking pockets and scavenging, but also, as Twig described it, by "going off with men."

"Rose was always in an' out of Bridewell," whispered Twig. "That's the last place I saw 'er, since we *Duty* boys were kept in that prison for a time afore we were shipped to Virginia."

"How did she manage to come to Virginia on the *Jonathan?*" Sarah wondered aloud. "The Virginia Company demanded church references from the brides."

"Most likely faked the ref'rences."

"Perhaps. Go on."

Twig hunched his shoulders under his thin blanket, then continued. "When I was real young—maybe five—Rose birthed a boy. Sickly it was. Cried most-a the time. Made Rose furious, that did, so sometimes she'd slap it."

Sarah's quiet groan filled the loft.

"One night, when we was huddled round a fire tryin' to get warm, the babe began to cry, and nothin' Rose did could make it hush."

Feeling him shiver, Sarah found her shawl and wrapped it around Twig's shoulders. "What happened?"

"She became fearful angry and went off toward the river. I was afeard for the wee 'un, so I followed her. I tried to hold Rose back when I saw what she plotted, but she was too strong. There was nothin' I could do." Twig took a deep breath, as though gathering courage to say what happened next, then whispered, "She threw the baby into the river."

Sarah's mind reeled from the horror of Twig's words. "I do not think the babe even 'ad a name," he finished quietly.

"Did you go to the authorities in London?" Sarah asked, reaching out to take Twig's small, cold hand in hers.

Twig shook his head. "No use. They wouldn't believe a beggar brat. And the babe, too, was a beggar's brat. One more or less makes no matter to 'em."

Sarah shuddered, even though the air was warm. "That's why you told us not to let Rose near Hannah. You were worried she'd hurt that infant, too. I don't think she would have. But what you said about Rose trying to poison Jacob—perhaps that wasn't so crazy after all."

"She has good reason to be rid of 'im." Twig leaned forward, his breath moist on Sarah's face. "He hits 'er."

"How do you know? He doesn't seem a gentle man, yet . . ."

"I've heard 'im. I sometimes stand outside their palisade and listen. Once I peeked through a crack." Twig paused. "That time 'e used a board. And Rose never made a sound. She didn't cry neither."

Sarah groaned and wrapped her arms around her shoulders.

"Before, I used to hate 'er. After that, I started to feel sorry for 'er. Not a lot, but a little." Twig plucked at Sarah's nightgown. "Ya gonna tell 'bout the baby?"

Sarah thought of Rose escaping to the New World, taking with her her horrible secret, hoping to find a new life and finding, instead, Jacob Howe.

Sarah put her arm around Twig's shoulders. "No. We're not going to tell. I gave you my promise. Besides, it's your word against hers, and you're a child—and an indentured servant. So telling would be no use."

Twig gave a small grunt, but Sarah couldn't tell if it was a grunt of approval or disapproval. The room was brightening, and she fixed her gaze on his and continued. "But just because there may not be enough proof to bring Rose to trial and have her punished isn't the reason we won't tell."

Twig's eyes widened.

"I think ... I think Rose has found punishment enough already."

Narrowing his eyes, Twig nodded. "Jacob?"

"Jacob."

"I'm glad we're not gonna tell."

For a moment Sarah sat quietly, a picture in her head of Rose flinging a tiny baby into the dark water of the Thames River. She shuddered, remembering how hard it had been to lay John's baby in the grave, even wrapped tightly in the arms of Hannah, his mother, even though he was already dead, had, in fact, never drawn breath. Sarah shook her head. *How could Rose do it? Kill her own child? How?*

At last Twig threw off his covers and slipped out from under Sarah's arm, as though out from under a heavy load. "Come on. It's near light, and today's the day we start toppin' the 'bacca. We can do yers and still be back in time fer the mornin' meal."

Sarah's mood was still gloomy as she turned her back, pulled her gown over her head and tucked up her hair. But finally Twig's relieved, eager spirit captured her, and she put sad thoughts of Rose and her murdered baby out of her mind.

"Now tell me, how do we top tobacco and why do we do it?" she whispered, as they climbed down the ladder.

At the bottom, Twig turned to her and raised his hands. "I thought you knew."

"I don't know. I thought you knew."

Twig pulled at his top lip. "I think Walter said it makes the leaves grow bigger and 'eavier."

"But how do you do it?" Sarah hissed.

"Count twenty-five or thirty leaves up from the bottom and lop off everything above that," rumbled Walter's voice from the bed, where he and Margaret slept. "Now scram before I rattle your teeth loose in your noggins."

With a squeak Twig scuttled toward the door, Sarah close behind.

Two days later Jacob came to tell Harwood that Rose had packed a bundle and fled into the forest. For three days the men searched, but no trace of her was found. Tongues wagged for weeks wondering what became of her. Perhaps she was taken by a wild animal. Perhaps she became mired in a swamp and drowned. Perhaps she was murdered by strange Indians.

"I 'spect Jacob killed and buried 'er," announced Twig to Sarah. "I bet she's blazin' in hell this very minute."

It would be nearly a year before they learned of Rose's true fate.

∽∽∽

Chapter 23

By June everyone in Wolstenholme Towne was working feverishly. Harwood had proven to be an able leader and was determined the colonists would have a bountiful crop of tobacco to take to the company store after curing time. He kept the men so busy that five or six natives, including Rawhunt, now lived in the settlement and did all the hunting and fishing. Some of the men had given other natives their muskets, so those Indians, too, hunted, leaving the settlers more time to work the fields.

"We are inviting disaster!" Richard fumed, adding that only a few months before, the King of the Eastern Shore, known as the Laughing King, had warned Governor Yeardley that the Indians were planning treachery.

"But didn't Opechancanough, the werowance, deny there was any plot?" asked Anne, who had come to visit Sarah and was now helping shell corn.

"Aye." Richard's voice was sharp, but his eyes, as they looked at Anne, had a soft light in them. "And the Indians have been so peaceful and cooperative since then, it's tempting to believe the wily old werowance," Richard continued. "But I think the chief's words are false."

"But only last month Opechancanough himself again said the sky would fall before the peace between the Indians and the white settlers dissolved," said John, who, since Hannah's death, often came to sit with the Davidsons, his face and shoulders drooping, his look so sad it made Sarah want to reach out and sweep away the lines rimming his eyes and mouth. "I believe Opechancanough speaks the truth," John added, rubbing his hands over the mottled maple knot he was carving into a bowl.

"But don't forget," Richard snapped, "that as a young man Opechancanough spent years in Spain, some of them at court, where he probably learned a great deal about the cunning art of currying trust from his enemies."

Here we go again, thought Sarah. *Will we ever discover something John and Richard agree on?* She started to nibble a thumbnail, but the bitter taste stopped her. After tutoring, she had hoed her tobacco and pinched off the suckers that tried to sprout between the stalk and the leaf stems, filling her nails with gummy black sap.

Sarah sighed. *I smell like tobacco and taste like it too,* she thought, wearily rubbing her face. *Unlike John and Richard, I am too tired to* have *an opinion, much less defend one.*

At least the tobacco was growing full and heavy, and it seemed her efforts would be worthwhile. But she looked forward to September, when the cutting would be finished and the tobacco hung on lines to cure. Even more, she anticipated the day when the cured tobacco would be delivered to the store and Sarah would hold in her hands her escape money. With only twenty plants, she wouldn't earn enough to pay her fare, but another year of tutoring and making soap ashes, and, if necessary, another crop of tobacco, might earn her enough, especially now that she had hoed hills for another thirty plants.

"Perhaps a year from now I'll be in England," Sarah had told Anne earlier that evening. Now, as she sat yawning among the guests, she realized she was even too tired to feel excited at the thought of going home.

At last the hard work of summer and autumn were done and the settlers felt prepared for whatever the coming winter might bring. In November, Francis Wyatt arrived on the *George* to replace Yeardley as governor. That month, too, Sarah's bundle of cured tobacco was taken to Jamestown. She received three shillings a pound, and looked at the English money in her hand with a mixture of pride and dismay. Pride because she had done it: She had claimed her land, planted tobacco, and earned money for her fare home. Dismay because she had learned that in 1614 the price of a pound of tobacco was ten shillings, and now, in 1621, it was three shillings, and there was talk of the price falling again—all because the harvest was a good one.

"The more plentiful the goods, the lower the price," Walter said, when Sarah asked for an explanation.

Soon after, the new governor announced that, in order to halt overproduction and end low prices, no one could grow more than one thousand tobacco plants, and each plant had to be topped to only nine leaves.

Sarah groaned. While she was a long way from having a thousand plants, at that leaf limit the fifty hills she now had would produce only a few more leaves than the twenty hills she had planted last summer. It seemed she had taken one step closer to England and one step away.

The *Warwick* came in December, bringing twenty-eight people for Martin's Hundred, including a few maids hoping to find husbands. That shouldn't take long, Sarah decided. The population of the settlement had grown to nearly one hundred, most of them unmarried men eager to find a wife. There had at times been many more, but death still stalked them; nearly seven out of every ten still died.

Sarah wasn't nearly as pleased to see the new people as she was to see the two cows, Daisy and Whiteface, that also came on the *Warwick*. She could nearly taste the cream as they staggered ashore, looking much as Sarah felt the first time she set her sea legs on Virginia soil.

There was little forage during the winter months, so the settlers fed the cows part of their precious grain supply, but that wasn't a worry. The people of Martin's Hundred were well-provisioned that winter. They even had a food new to the north.

"It's called a patate," John explained to Rawhunt, holding up a tuber that was nearly as long as Twig's leg. "There are red patates and white patates, and they taste good boiled."

That day in January 1622, when John introduced Rawhunt to potatoes, was one Sarah would remember, for it was the first time John and Richard found something they agreed on.

John had arrived at the Davidsons' carrying a basket filled with oysters two hands wide. Now, as John was showing Rawhunt the potato, Richard arrived, the stomp of his feet announcing his mood before he appeared.

Before anyone could speak, Richard pointed his finger in Rawhunt's face, an action John had told Sarah the Indians thought very rude. "You and the others are still taking the boats without permission!"

For some weeks the natives had been borrowing the settlement boats to travel up and down the river to visit other tribes. At first they asked permission. Now they didn't bother.

Richard turned his gaze toward John. "Have you noticed how much more neighborly they've become in the past while?" he muttered under his breath, so Rawhunt wouldn't hear. "Do you still think they plan no treachery?"

"I do." John tossed the potato he still held to Rawhunt, who had been standing quietly, a nearly invisible twitch next to his right eye the only hint of how he felt about Richard's finger-pointing or his words.

"But I agree about the boats," John continued. He rested his hand on Rawhunt's shoulder. "This morning I had to walk to the oyster beds, then use the rickety raft left there," he told his friend. "Unless you're fishing for the settlement, it is best if you ask before taking the boats."

"It is best if they don't take the boats at all, with or without consent!" Richard fixed a fierce look on Rawhunt, as though that alone would make the entire tribe of natives comply, then stalked off.

"I don't think Harwood will refuse you the boats as long as you ask first," John told Rawhunt when Richard was gone. "But tell the others they must ask, or Lieutenant Kean might convince Harwood to deny permission."

Rawhunt had nodded slowly, then gone off.

"I'll see you later this evening," John told Sarah. "Walter has invited me to play a game of put with him. Perhaps you'll join us?"

Twig had trotted up in time to hear John's invitation. "Ya don't want her to play. She's 'opeless at cards." He pulled himself tall and straightened his shirt. "Me now, I'm a champion put player."

Sarah gave Twig a light rap on his head. "No doubt you learned it from some street beggar."

Twig nodded. "Not much else to do on a winter's night when it's too cold to sleep and there're no pockets 'round to pick."

John looked at Sarah, his eyebrows raised. She looked down at her hands, which were twisting the handle of the oyster basket. "Let Twig play," she mumbled. "I have a pile of mending to do." Then she shook a finger at the boy. "And I know one young lad who'd better hope I don't sew the legs of his ripped breeches together."

With a giggle, Twig ran off to feed the chickens.

Sarah thanked John for the oysters, then boldly asked, "Do you realize you and Richard just agreed with each other?"

For a brief moment John looked puzzled, then slapped his thigh. "About the borrowing. You're right. We did. It must be the season for miracles."

Indeed it is, Sarah thought, as the two stood grinning at each other. *It's the first time that I have truly felt at ease alone with a man, and the first time since Hannah's death that I've seen John smile.*

Chapter 24

When John arrived at the Davidsons' that evening for his game of put, grief seemed once again to have settled on him. Sarah couldn't bear to see his unhappy look, so she set aside her mending, grabbed her cloak, and slipped quietly out the door.

A full moon gilded a path to where the maple's bare limbs etched black against the sooty sky. Quickly Sarah followed it, then climbed the tree until she was safe on her perch.

Moments later the palisade gate banged. Were the guests leaving so soon, or had Margaret missed her and sent Twig looking? A quiet voice rose on the cold January air.

"I know you still grieve for Hannah and the wee one," Margaret said, and Sarah realized John was with her. "But I think more than that is troubling you. I insist you tell me what it is. After all, we've known each other for many years, and I like to think us more than friends."

Sarah knew Margaret's father had farmed the land next to the Clark family farm in Surrey. "Margaret's father was an honest yeoman of the country and quite wealthy," John had said one evening when the Clarks and Sarah were visiting Anne and Cisly. "But he had a savage temper. Margaret was his only daughter, and when she married Walter, Margaret's father was outraged because Walter was only a poor tenant farmer on Mister Jones's land. Her father felt Margaret had married below her station. He was so angry he knocked out her teeth and cast her off from the family."

Sarah had shivered at his words, just as she now shivered in the chill winter air. She pulled her cloak more tightly about her, remembering.

"Is that why she came to Virginia?" Hannah had asked John.

"Aye. Margaret and Walter farmed her father's land for years after the wedding, but her father never spoke to Margaret again. So at last the two of them came here, where someday they hope Walter will become a wealthy landowner and they can prove her father wrong."

"What a sad story," Anne had said. Sarah, thinking back, as she sat perched in her moonlit maple, agreed.

Margaret and John stopped near the tree. "You and I *are* friends." John's voice was quiet, but Sarah could hear him clearly, and she wondered if she should speak, should let them know she was there, so they wouldn't think she was spying on them. Then she thought how foolish she would feel, for in two months she would be sixteen. Young ladies of nearly sixteen did not climb trees in the daytime, much less in the dark. She held her breath and sat quietly, determined not to be discovered.

"You're wrong. I'm not grieving for Hannah," John said, "and that's why I mourn."

"I don't understand." Sarah imagined Margaret's eyebrows bunched together as she looked at John.

"I grieved for the son I never knew, but I have not grieved for Hannah as she deserved because ... I ... I did not love her as she deserved." John's voice broke.

Sarah let out a small gasp, but the two didn't look up. John didn't love Hannah? She didn't want to hear this! Suddenly Sarah wished she had hallooed down the tree and made her presence known.

Sarah saw Margaret reach out a hand and rest it on John's arm. "You were always kind and gentle with her. It did seem as though you loved her."

"I tried. Heaven knows I tried. But I could not. I . . . I liked her, yes. I admired her . . . her courage, her industry. She was such a . . . decent soul. She deserved better than I gave her."

"And the guilt is eating at you."

"You don't know what a burden it places on a person not to love a mate," John said, his voice a broken whisper. "You wed the one you loved, in spite of the consequences."

Margaret patted John's shoulder. "You were a good husband to Hannah. Don't flog yourself for marrying her without loving her. That's the way with most marriages. With life so uncertain, there isn't time to let love grow beforehand. We must get on with the living."

Margaret took John's face between her hands and gave his head a gentle shake. "No man should be single if he can find a wife to do for him. Find a new mate and get on with your life."

"But Hannah is scarcely cold in her grave!" John protested.

"It's nearly a year," Margaret said, her stern voice rising in crisp tones to Sarah's numbing ears. "Besides, most men outlive their wives. In this country they often outlive a number of wives, for the work is hard and bearing children harder. Jacob Mason in Henrico is on his sixth wife now, if the tales I hear are true. Walter told me people were consoling Master Mason on the death of his last wife and congratulating him on his choice for his new one at the same time."

John's groan lifted upward to where Sarah sat clutching the trunk of the tree as a sailor clutches the mast of a sinking ship. "That would only be repeating my mistake a second time."

Margaret gave a *tsk* of annoyance, and Sarah could tell the older woman was sucking her lower lip into her mouth. "Surely, there's one unmarried woman in the settlement you care for, even a little, or at least one you might come to care for." Margaret was silent for a moment, then quietly said words that made Sarah's icy cheeks burn. "Sarah will be sixteen in March. She's of an age to marry—and I know you're friends."

A cry of disbelief sprang to Sarah's lips, but she managed to stifle it, and pressed her cheek hard against the tree, wondering if she would singe the bark, her head felt so fiery. Of an age to marry? She, Sarah? Of an age to marry? Her brain pounded against her skull as though wanting to be free. She and John? Man and wife? She clutched the tree harder for fear she would faint and plummet to the ground at John's feet. Marry John and be tied to Virginia forever? *Never,* she wanted to scream at the figures below. Never!

John's voice drifted upward, muffled by the ringing in Sarah's ears. "Sarah is special. And you're right; we have become good friends. She was a good friend to Hannah and is a good friend to me. But I'm still an indentured servant. I don't believe Sarah would marry a servant."

"Your indenture is up when? A year from this month? That's not much of a hindrance to happiness."

"Aye, one year. Then I'm a free man again." John took a breath so deep it sounded to Sarah as though he sucked air all the way down to his toes before he blew it out. "But you know, it's whispered that Sarah is biding her time in this land until she can pay her way back to England, and that is why she works so hard on her tobacco and her soap ashes.''

"She doesn't speak of it, but I've heard the whispers, too,'' Margaret said. "I say nothing to her, because I keep hoping she'll come to love this country and choose to stay. Sarah is good for Virginia. She'd be good for you, too.''

John kicked his toe into the dirt, the boot making a dull thunk, thunk in the quiet night. "I'll think about your advice. We'll see what happens.''

As John and Margaret started back toward the house, Sarah sat silently hugging the tree, wishing she had never eavesdropped on their conversation, and wondering how she could ever again be at ease in John's presence.

∽∾∽

Chapter 25

Sarah could not meet Margaret's gaze during the days that followed and took great care to avoid John. What would she say and how would she act when they came face to face? Would she blush and look foolish, the way she used to whenever a man spoke to her? Would John study her every move like a gypsy at a horse fair studies a mare he hopes to buy? she wondered, hurrying quickly from task to task, as though each step were an embarrassing thought she wanted to leave behind. Then early one evening, while she was home alone, a knock came at the door. When Sarah answered, John was standing there.

Sarah's face grew warm. She willed herself to be calm as he greeted her, reminding herself that John didn't know she had overheard his conversation with Margaret.

"I haven't seen you for a while," John said, "and I remember you saying I could borrow your copy of Ovid's *Metamorphoses*."

Sarah's serenity fled. Her teeth found a fingernail she hadn't yet chewed. "Did you hear that George Sandys is continuing to translate the work while he's living in

Jamestown?'' she said, her voice thin and squeaky around her finger.

When John shook his head, she rapidly prattled on. ''Now that I've read the Latin, I should like to read his translation to see how it compares. I would have purchased copies of his first five volumes before I left England, but I had no money to buy them and no room to carry them.''

Be still! Sarah shouted silently, as her tongue wagged on, but her tongue didn't listen. ''It's a fine thing, is it not, that our treasurer in Jamestown is such a learned scholar?'' At last Sarah's tongue lay quiet, but the uncomfortable silence that followed wound itself around her like a clammy ship's sail that had come loose from its mooring.

John's eyes opened wide and he muttered some sort of reply, before Sarah stumbled off to find her book, her knees nearly knocking together, her skirts tangling about her feet.

Idiot! she scolded herself as she scrambled up the ladder to the loft, where her chests were stored. *As far as John knows, nothing has changed. Act the way you've always acted with him, or he'll think you've gone daft.*

Oh! Sarah thought, *if he thinks I'm daft he won't be interested in me. Then things can go back to the way they were before ... before I spied on him and Margaret.*

Oh no, if I act daft he'll guess that I did spy. Or else he'll accuse Margaret of telling me, and she'll guess I spied. I must act natural. I must ... act ... natural.

She was still trying to calm her heart and quiet her thoughts when she heard Anne call below. ''Margaret! Where is she?''

''She's at the compound, tending the men who are

ill," John answered, for the dying had once again arrived with the new year.

"What's happened?" Sarah asked, hurrying down the ladder, all her fretful thoughts gone.

"Cisly," was all Anne said, as she ran toward the gate in the palisade. John followed, the book forgotten. When, after a short time, no one returned, Sarah started after them, only to meet Twig on the gully path.

"Mistress Davidson says come. She hasn't enough hands ta see ta all who're ill, and Anne'll need yer help."

"Help with what?"

"Cisly is sick." Twig grabbed Sarah by the hand and tugged. "Yer ta hurry. Anne says Cisly's dyin'."

Sarah's stomach clenched as though a giant fist had taken hold of it and squeezed. "That can't be true. Cisly is stronger than all of us. Many fall ill, but he goes on as ever."

"No more," Twig said, giving Sarah a push along the path toward the Mills's.

When Sarah reached Anne's house, she saw Cisly had lost much resemblance to the sturdy man who had claimed Anne's heart. His skin was pulled so tight across his face even his freckles seemed drained of their color. Cisly's breath was fleeting and ragged, his body now and again shaken by huge racking coughs that would seem to tear it into shreds. His babbling made no sense.

Margaret was with him. John had come, too, and was setting water on the fire to boil.

"The sickness came so quickly," said Anne, who was seated at Cisly's head, wiping his brow. "Only last night, and then it was only a small fever."

Margaret rested her hand on Anne's shoulder. "I don't know what pestilence this is, but these plagues often come like that. One moment a man will be walking around, perfectly fine, the next ..." She shook her head.

Sarah knew Margaret was thinking of Thomas Miller, who had bid Walter good morning a few weeks ago, had taken a couple more steps—and dropped dead.

"I must go back to those in the compound," she said then, turning to Sarah. "You'll have to do what you can for him. We have no roasted onion to fill with treacle and pepper, nor any figs to give him. But here is some dried rue and a few blanched walnuts beaten small. Try to get him to take some. And give him an infusion of tobacco to purge the sour humors that rack his body. I'm afraid it's all we can do."

Margaret brushed a hand gently down Anne's hair. "Help if you can," she told her, "although the comfort you bring him simply by being near will probably do as much as my medicines will.

"And you ..." Margaret turned to John. "You best leave, unless you can be of some help."

"I can," said John, and turned back to the fire.

Sarah was glad of the numbness she felt as she went about the tasks Margaret had set, for the dying Cisly was a gruesome sight to behold.

Anne bathed Cisly's face and hands. John tried to force some rue and beaten walnuts into his mouth, while Sarah made up the infusion. Then John propped Cisly up, and Anne held his head, while Sarah poured the liquid between his parched lips.

Some time later the infusion began to do its duty. Rivulets of sweat poured off Cisly. He began to vomit, and soon the purging of his bowels began. At last it was over, and they cleaned up the mess their attempted remedies had wrought.

Anne gently laid her hand on Cisly's cheek. "Better to let him die peacefully than repeat this torture." But then she leaned over and whispered loudly in her hus-

149

band's ear, "You must live, Cisly, for come summer, you will be a father. I know how much you hope for a child, and I was waiting to be sure before I told you."

While she spoke, Anne continued to pat Cisly's cheek. "I should have told you when you first got sick, but that was only last night." She looked at Sarah, then at John, her eyes brilliant with unshed tears. "He doesn't know. He doesn't know he's to be a father."

Quickly John knelt beside Anne and took her hand in his. "He knows. Only the other day he told me of his suspicions, but he didn't want to spoil your surprise. He was very proud, Anne."

Anne looked thoughtful, then, for a brief second, her face lit up. "Before he began to rave, he said, 'Don't wear yourself out fussing over me. You must begin to take better care of yourself now.' " She smiled a wisp of a smile. "He did know, didn't he?" As Anne spoke those words, Cisly began to cough again, and it seemed as though every cough would split open his chest and spill his innards on the bed. Anne's anxious look reappeared.

"I think something to ease his cough would be wise," Sarah said. She set about collecting sage and cumin, which she dusted with pepper, before adding a pinch of Margaret's rue and some boiled honey.

After they forced a spoonful of the mixture between Cisly's clenched teeth, Sarah stepped out into the night, where she stood for a long while, taking deep breaths to rid herself of the reek of death. The air was crisp on her cheek, and she didn't want to go in again, but when at last she did, Cisly lay quiet, though his breath rattled in his chest. He did not cough again before he died.

When she saw he was dead, Anne looked at Sarah, her eyes blue pools of pain, her freckles standing forth against her pale face. "He would have made a wonderful father." Then tears spilled from her eyes, and she laid her head on Cisly's chest and let them flow.

When Anne's sobbing had eased, John told her, "It was fever, so he must be buried tonight. I'm afraid there'll be no time to build a coffin."

Anne, her eyes red-rimmed, her cheeks blotchy, looked at Sarah. "Please, will you help me prepare him?"

Sarah had no heart for what Anne asked, but she couldn't say no to her friend. John poured some hot water into a wooden basin, and Sarah found two rags. Then, while John went off to dig a grave in the cemetery overlooking the river, Anne and Sarah washed Cisly's body and wrapped him in clean linen.

An icy rain was falling as they buried Cisly, along with two others who had died. Then the rain turned to snow. Soon the raw, wounded earth was covered with soft white.

But still Sarah felt the rain within her heart, within her soul, and she well imagined the sadness of her friend, the emptiness of her house. So, when Margaret tried to convince Anne to come home with them, and Anne refused, Sarah stayed with her.

They couldn't bring themselves to sleep in the bed where Cisly died, so they made a pallet of corn shucks on the floor and slept there. Only the steadiness of the floor and the memories they had since claimed as their own, memories both happy and sad, made that night different from the nights they had slept huddled together on the *Jonathan* so many months before.

Bleak winter day followed bleak winter day, and still Sarah stayed on with Anne. After a couple of weeks, she had Walter bring over her chests and made the move permanent. Then one day Twig arrived with a bundle, and announced, "I told Margaret you two need a man 'bout the house. Besides, one of those silly chits who came on the *Warwick,* Jane Fiske, 'as moved into the house while she tries ta catch herself a husband. That shouldn't take long, the way she flirts. But she's always tryin' ta get me ta do 'er work for 'er. So I've come ta stay.''

So Twig moved in too, spending most of each day helping Walter or Margaret, but always arriving for supper. Sarah suspected he ate with the Davidsons and then scurried back to eat with her and Anne. Fortunately there was no shortage of food that winter, for Twig's appetite was enormous, and he ate more than Anne and Sarah together. But still he stayed his same scrawny self, if possible becoming leaner as he became longer.

The three of them seemed a sort of family—working, playing, nagging, and scolding. While Anne's sorrow didn't fully fade, and Sarah often saw her kneeling in the cold dirt by Cisly's grave, her giggle occasionally filled the house. Then Sarah and Twig would look at each other and grin.

The first time Sarah saw John after Cisly died, she realized the awkward feelings she had had were gone. Cisly's death made her worries seem paltry, and she was almost ashamed to recall the panic she had felt after she had eavesdropped on John and Margaret. For the first time since she came to Virginia, she felt serene, peaceful.

One evening, while she was brushing Anne's hair and watching Twig attempt to whittle a spoon, she realized why. At first she wanted to push the thought aside, told herself she was imagining it. But finally she had to admit that, now, at last, in spite of so much tragedy, she felt at home.

Suddenly London with its busy shops, its faceless crowds, its clattery cobblestoned streets, its Westminster

Abbey, its Bloody Tower, its sooty air, was a part of Sarah's past.

She tried to picture herself walking the streets among the throngs of people, apprenticing for a seamstress, renting a room in someone's home. She saw, instead, rows of lush tobacco plants, a wattle-and-daub cottage with smoke rising from the chimney, the noonday sun turning the James to a silver ribbon, a V-shaped wedge of geese against a crimson sky, cardinals busy about their nests, the soft yellow of tiny butterflowers thrusting hopefully upward. She saw, instead, Virginia.

At that moment Twig looked at her with a cocked-head grin, and Anne reached up, took the hairbrush from Sarah's hand, and said, "Now I'll brush yours." At that moment Sarah knew she could never leave them, knew she had come home.

☙❧

Chapter 26

January gave way to February, with its hesitant hints of spring, then to March, with its bold promise. One day Margaret marched to Anne's door, her lips drawn thin, a determined look on her face. Scowling at Anne, she said, "You must choose a husband. You've been discouraging suitors from calling. But you need a man to care for you and to be a father to that babe you're carrying. Stop dillydallying and make a choice." She scratched an ear and added, "Best do your pickin' while the pickin's good. Besides, it's not seemly, two unmarried women living alone among so many men, with only a boy to watch out for them." She turned and stomped off, calling over her shoulder, "I'm going to spread the word: Widow Mills is open to offers."

Anne had a pained look when she turned to Sarah. "It's only been two months and I'm not ready to marry again, but I know she's right." She ran her hands over her stomach, which was just beginning to swell, sighed, and sank onto a stool. "I know my baby needs a father. But I feel as though I'd be betraying Cisly."

Sarah rested a hand on Anne's shoulder. "I think Cisly would want you and his child to be taken care of. Perhaps you should choose a husband."

Anne's brow wrinkled. "What about you? Why didn't Margaret tell you it's time to find a husband? Goodness, you'll be sixteen in a few weeks, nearly the same age I was when I came here."

"I . . . I . . . suppose . . . It might be that . . ." Sarah studied the feathered turkey wing she'd been using to sweep the hearth. "Perhaps Margaret thinks I'm still planning to return to England."

Leaping to her feet, Anne stuck her face in Sarah's and said, "That sounds as though Margaret thinks wrong. Aren't you still planning to go home? Are you, instead, thinking of staying in Virginia—with me?" Anne's red eyebrows were raised marks of anticipation.

Slowly Sarah nodded.

With a squeal, Anne flung her arms around Sarah. "Oh, I have prayed so long, so hard for this day, even harder since Cisly died." And she burst into tears.

"Then you can choose a husband, too," Anne said, when her tears had dried.

Sarah shook her head. "I'm not the timid girl I was two years ago, but I still don't feel ready to marry. Perhaps in another year . . ." She chuckled. "Besides, what if you and I wanted the same man? Would we still be best of friends?"

Anne laughed, too, then became serious. "Neither man nor beast would stop me from being your friend. Now tell me about the available men in the settlement. I've not paid much attention these past two years."

Sarah rattled off names and descriptions of the unmarried men in Martin's Hundred. "But I know one who is already in love with you and has been for some time," she said, when she finished. "No doubt he'll be knocking at the door as soon as Margaret spreads her news."

"And who is that?"

"Richard Kean."

Anne's face turned cardinal red. "I supposed as much. Cisly even used to tease that Richard might be lucky enough to be a lieutenant, but he wasn't lucky enough to be Anne's husband." A lone tear escaped and slid down her cheek.

Sarah waved her hand in the air. "Oh, don't worry about Richard. You can always refuse him, just as you did on board ship that time."

Anne smiled a rueful smile. "The time I called him the tail of the gentry." She swiped at the wandering tear with the back of her hand, and sighed. "Richard's not as pompous as we thought. Of course, he still takes his job *so* seriously. But it's a good job, and we'd be well-provided for. I could do worse than to marry Richard." She sighed again and patted her stomach. "But would he accept Cisly's child?"

Right then, Twig stuck his head in the door. "Margaret's goin' about tellin' all that yer searchin' fer a husband. And just now I heard ya talkin' 'bout Lieutenant Kean." His small face fell. "If ya marry Lieutenant Kean, I'll not be able ta visit ya, for he looks down 'is nose at me."

Sarah's heart clenched at the wistful note in Twig's voice. She pulled him inside. "Who says she's marrying Lieutenant Kean?"

"Whenever Lieutenant Kean's around, he's always castin' hungry puppy-dog looks her way."

Anne knelt beside Twig. "You can come and visit me, even dine with me, whenever you want, no matter who I marry."

Twig's thin body sagged with relief. He grinned. "If it's Lieutenant Kean, I shall hafta mind me manners and not slobber on me chin, else he'll put the flat of his sword to me hind parts." With a giggle, he was gone.

That evening Richard did come to call, looking very handsome in the blue silk doublet and breeches he had worn upon his arrival at Jamestown nearly two years before.

Except for his clothing, Richard gave no hint that he had come courting. In fact, the evening passed as had any evening before Cisly died, with Twig groaning over a piece of carving wood, the women mending, and the visitor quietly puffing on his pipe and occasionally commenting on the weather and the Indians. Richard did little to remind them of the haughty man who had called Anne a person of lesser quality. If Richard remembered that she, in turn, had called him the tail of the gentry, he made no mention of it.

"Hunger, sickness, and danger are great equalizers," Anne said, after Richard had gone. "I think Lieutenant Kean has come to realize that under the skin we're all the same."

" 'Lessen yer talkin' 'bout Injuns," Twig piped up.

"Unless we're talking about Indians," Anne agreed with a laugh.

"On that subject Lieutenant Kean has much to learn," Sarah added.

Although other men came visiting in the days that followed, no one was more faithful than Richard, though his attempts at flirtation were hopelessly inept and the cause of much joking between Sarah and Twig.

"Oh, Mistress Mills," Twig would mimic Richard when the man had gone. "You look particularly . . . particularly . . . um . . . particularly fetching . . . yes, fetching this evening."

"Why, thank you, kind sir," Sarah would joke, tugging bashfully at a hank of her hair and fluttering her eyelashes. "Your blue silk—which you've appeared in every evening for a week, and which dreadfully needs a good brushing—looks as . . . um . . . as . . . fetching . . . yes, as fetching on you as ever."

"You're being unkind," Anne told them one night

after Richard had stammered his way through a number of botched compliments. "The man has spent his life in foreign lands with scarcely a woman in sight. He's doing the best he can."

After that, Sarah and Twig kept their jokes to themselves. Then, one evening, as he was preparing to leave, Richard asked, "May I have a private word with you, Anne?" And he drew her out the door into the moonlight.

Twig scampered to the window and peeped out through a gap in the wooden shutter.

"Get away from there." Sarah tugged at his shirttail, but Twig pulled free and waved his hand at her to be quiet.

The couple must not have gone far from the door, because Sarah could hear Richard's voice quite plainly. "It's a . . . a fine evening," he stammered.

Sarah couldn't resist. She, too, was overcome with curiosity. She turned and quickly blew out the candle burning nearby, then crept to the window and squinted out.

Richard was staring at the toe of his boot and fumbling with the hilt of his sword. Anne was standing next to him, examining the sky as though she had never seen a full moon before.

Suddenly Richard was down on one knee before her, heedless of the damp ground. Anne gave a small start of amazement.

"It has been two years since first I asked for your hand, and you refused me," Richard said, gazing at Anne's shoes. "Instead, you married Cisly. But he's dead, and come summer, you are to bear a child, who will need a father. So I find my chance has come again." Richard raised his head and looked into Anne's face. "Marry me, Anne, and I will make you smile once more."

Sarah choked back a giggle, wondering how a man who seldom smiled himself could make Anne smile, and remembering how once she had thought that *Anne* could teach *Richard* to laugh and be jolly. Well, no doubt she would. It might take a while, until Anne stopped mourning Cisly and became her old, happy self again, but Sarah knew Anne would be good for Richard.

She wondered what it would be like, married to Richard. *Would he ask his wife to salute him?* she mused, nearly giggling aloud. No doubt, Mistress Kean would have to become accustomed to sleeping with a sword between her and her husband. Sarah was about to share her humorous thoughts with Twig, when she had a sobering one. Anne and Cisly had been so much alike, if one had grown more like the other, no one would have noticed. But Richard was so different from Cisly—and from Anne. What if, instead of Richard becoming less rigid, Anne grew more like him? What if Richard turned Anne into an arrogant, humorless person like himself? Her friend would be lost to her. Suddenly Anne marrying Richard didn't seem like such a good idea. *Say no,* Sarah begged silently.

But even in the moonlight Sarah could see the beseeching look in Richard's eye and saw how willingly he knelt before Anne in the mud, and her sudden doubts faded. All the miseries of the past two years swarmed before her eyes, the last being the still, pale face of Cisly. She thought how comforting it would be for Anne to have someone with whom to share the pain of future tragedies, because one thing the years had taught Sarah—there was no life without tragedy.

Anne drew Richard to his feet. "I'm honored," she told him. "I'll not refuse you a second time. I will be your wife."

The look of joy on Richard's usually stern face nearly outshone the moon. "And when the baby comes," he said, taking Anne's hand, "feel free to honor Cisly's memory by giving it his surname. However, I would also be honored if you choose, instead, to give it mine."

If Richard had been standing beside her, Sarah believed she would have hugged him. Instead, she put her arm around Twig's thin shoulders and gave him a squeeze.

Twig shrugged off Sarah's arm and turned to her with a teasing smirk. "Be ya jealous?"

Sarah aimed a cuff at his head, but he was too quick, and ducked. "Light the candle," she hissed, "or Anne will know we were spying on them." But as she returned to her mending, Sarah had a new, unfamiliar longing in her heart.

Anne set the wedding date for the following week, March 22, 1622. "That's Good Friday and your sixteenth birthday, Sarah," Anne announced. "It can't help but be a lucky day."

But one evening, Richard arrived in a turmoil, and it seemed the wedding might have to be postponed. "We've just learned Master Morgan was killed last week by an Indian called Nemattanow," he explained.

"That's the one we call Jack o' the Feathers, 'cause he goes round covered with so many feathers and swan wings," Twig announced.

"The boy's right. The natives also thought we English couldn't kill this Indian, that he was immortal." Wearily, Richard rubbed his hand along his jaw, then continued. "But now a bondsman of Morgan's *has* killed Nemattanow, and Opechancanough is speaking of revenge. Governor Wyatt has sent an emissary to the werowance to warn him against taking any action against us."

"What will happen?" asked Sarah, wondering what John must be thinking of all this.

"We must pray that Governor Wyatt's warning will be heeded," Richard answered.

160

The warning was heeded and the wedding was on again. Opechancanough again gave his assurance that the peace would not be broken. The very next week the *Concord* sailed for England carrying a letter from the governor of the Virginia Company. In it, Governor Wyatt wrote that the peace between the natives of Virginia and the English settlers was soundly concluded and faithfully kept.

But on the night before his wedding, Richard was still fretting. "I don't trust the werowance. He's devious and conniving. And if Wyatt trusts him, then Wyatt's a fool."

Anne patted Richard's arm. "Surely you're not going to be worrying about the natives tomorrow," she said, "the day I'm to become your wife."

Richard narrowed his eyes at Anne, but the angry glint in them was gone. "The safety of the settlement is in my hands," he said, "so, yes, I will be worrying about the natives tomorrow." Then, to Sarah's amazement, Richard grinned a broad grin that completely changed his appearance, before adding, "But only with a small corner of my mind. A very small corner."

"It's working," Sarah teased her friend after Richard had gone and they were preparing for bed. "Richard's hard shell is cracking. You might turn him into a human being after all."

"If his fierce Indians don't get him first," said Anne, but Sarah couldn't tell if she was joking or serious.

"Aw, he'll worry hisself to death 'fore any old Injun gets 'im," snorted Twig from his bed in the corner. Laughing, all three snuggled down—Twig to dream of being chased by an Indian covered with feathers; Anne to dream of marrying a man with two heads, one Richard's and one Cisly's; and Sarah to dream of getting stuck in her maple tree and missing the wedding.

Only Anne's dream didn't come true.

CRCRCR

Chapter 27

Early the next morning, just as the rays of the sun were seeping over the horizon to herald the start of that Good Friday, Sarah followed the path leading toward the Davidsons'. Moments later, she settled herself upon a large branch of her maple and looked down over Wolstenholme Towne, glad the swelling maple buds didn't block her view.

The town below had changed only a little since Sarah's arrival two years before. The church and barn were finished. There were a few more dwelling houses, one, the new house Richard had built for himself and Anne on the far side of the company compound. There were more fields to plant, more animals to tend, a few more people to work, a few more Indians coming and going. But little else was different.

Across the clearing, Twig scurried out of the path Sarah had just followed and headed for the Davidsons'. *No doubt looking for a second breakfast,* laughed Sarah, smoothing the skirt of her gray wool gown over her knees and pulling her shawl more tightly around her shoulders.

It was March 22, 1622—Anne's wedding day, Sarah's sixteenth birthday. She looked to the west, where her land lay waiting for the spring planting, and such a bubble of pride filled her that she feared she would float off her branch. *I love Virginia,* she admitted to herself for the first time. *Like Twig, it has squirmed its way into my heart.*

For a few minutes she dreamed about the day she could build a house and live on her land, but then she shook her head. *I came here to think about the changes today will bring,* she reminded herself.

"You and Twig can't live here alone," Richard had told her the night before. "Anne and I will be moving into our new house immediately, and I can't be responsible for your safety if you stay on here. After the wedding, you'll move back to the Davidsons'."

Sarah sighed. She had enjoyed living with Anne. Now she and Twig would be sleeping in the loft once again, and this time they would be sharing it with that husband-hungry—but very choosy—Jane Fiske. *If it weren't for that, life would be perfect,* Sarah thought.

Spark and Swad the oxen, their heads hanging over their stall door, lowed when a figure emerged from the longhouse, a bundle of tools over one shoulder. Sarah's stomach lurched when she recognized John. Her stomach had been doing that a lot lately. It was as though she were looking at John with new eyes, knowing John might be looking at her the same way. A year from now, when John was a free man and Sarah was seventeen, perhaps ... She kept her eyes on John as he walked along the track to the fort and disappeared inside.

Smoke slowly rose from chimneys, as people began to cook their morning meals. Sarah sniffed, but couldn't tell what Margaret had simmering, because the wind blew the scent away from her.

Rawhunt and Camohan crossed the field toward the Davidsons', Rawhunt carrying a goose over his shoulder. Already the birds were leaving, so the goose was likely the last fresh one Margaret would cook until the autumn brought them honking back.

A short time later, a few people left their houses and plodded toward the nearby fields. Twig scurried out of the Davidsons', the tweeting of his carved whistle fading into the woods, as he went to check Walter's turkey trap for any fowl careless enough to be lured into it. More Indians emerged from the forest and entered the homes of the Boyses, the Cumbers, the Snows, where the hunters often shared the morning meal they helped provide.

Pot lids banged, sleepy voices murmured, wash water sloshed out a doorway. *A few minutes more,* Sarah told herself, enjoying the morning sounds, *then I'll climb down. If I'm going to help Anne wash her hair and bathe before her wedding, I can't stay here much longer.* But Sarah didn't wish to leave the peace of her high perch, for she had decided it would be the last time she climbed the maple. Grown women don't climb trees, she had told herself, and, at sixteen, with a monthly flow and breasts, one surely is a woman. She leaned her cheek against the tree and felt the rough bark pressed beneath it.

Jane squawked, and Sarah raised her head with a smile. No doubt Margaret had asked Jane to stir the porridge and not to filtch a lick from the pot. Twig said Jane was as lazy as ever.

Sarah was still smiling when an Indian whoop echoed around the settlement, and moments later, cries began to shatter the morning peace, cries of pain and terror.

Sarah looked around in confusion, but nothing seemed changed. She shook her head, as though to clear her hearing. Then, at the house nearest her tree, Master Boys staggered into his yard, his head bloodied. An Indian followed, beating him with an ax. Master Boys fell, and the Indian went back into the house. Almost immediately, Mistress Boys shrieked, and her baby screamed.

Suddenly Sarah knew what was happening, and she cowered against the tree trunk in helpless horror. Richard had been right: Opechancanough had lied. The Indians were killing the settlers.

Anne! Sarah thought, as more screams split the morning air. *She's alone.* A charge raced through Sarah, like a bolt of lightning hurtling down her spine, and she made a move to climb down the tree. But another shriek stopped her, made her want to crawl beneath the bark of the maple, to stay above the horror, to stay safe. So, hating her helplessness, hating the fear that kept her there, Sarah simply sat on her limb and prayed as her friends and neighbors died.

She saw Christopher Guillam and Thomas Combar, who had been working in the field with three bondsmen, raise their heads at the first cries of alarm. Now they fled toward their homes, their families. Had they held onto their hoes, or even stayed together, they might have lived. But an Indian sprang upon Christopher from behind a shed and drove a knife into his heart. Thomas made it to his house and inside. He didn't come out again, and moments later, two Indians left the house, pausing only to set it on fire.

The cries had aroused the few men inside the fort, and Sarah saw their heads appear above the palisade. But most of the Indians stayed near the houses, out of musket range, so there was little those men could do.

William James stepped out the door of the longhouse and was struck down with a spade, then scalped. Sarah closed her eyes, bile choking her, her head swirling. Knowing if she fainted she would fall to her death, she lowered her shawl to her waist, and moving as little as possible, knotted it around the trunk of the tree. She was high above the attackers, and her gray gown blended with the bark of the maple, but it and all the trees around her were bare and open.

Sarah longed to close her eyes and sleep, hoping to wake and find it was all one of Twig's bad dreams. But her gaze was drawn downward with a horrid fascination she didn't understand.

Where was Richard? she wondered. Why hadn't he appeared to rally the people and defend the town? Where were all the muskets and the fine armor he was so proud of? WHAT WAS TAKING HIM SO LONG? It seemed as though the bloodshed had been going on for hours, yet it was only a few minutes since the first screams rent the air.

At last Richard appeared outside his new house, dressed only in his breeches, his musket in his hand, his sword at his side. An Indian was laying a burning pine knot to the longhouse thatch. Richard raised the musket and fired. The shot went wide, and the native crept inside the compound palisade.

Richard looked toward the fort, perhaps thinking to race toward it and its store of weapons. Then he looked toward the forest, and instead of going to the fort, he drew his sword and ran toward the company compound. Bellowing like a bull, he charged through the gate near the potter's shed and into the yard, intending, Sarah realized, to cut through it and on across the gully toward Anne's.

Not that way, Richard, Sarah thought, when she saw what awaited him. *Not that way.* Ashamed that she had not enough courage to call out to him, she lapsed into silence.

"ANNE!" Richard bawled as he came through the gate near the potter's shed. "A-A-A-A-A-A-NNE!"

The Indian crouching by the shed raised his iron spade, and as Richard ran past, brought it crashing down on Richard's forehead. Richard dropped. The Indian crushed the lieutenant's skull with a blow to the back of his head. The noise rose faintly to where Sarah sat, and she began to shake as if she had taken a chill. Her teeth rattled together like a woodpecker beating staccato upon a tree trunk. Then she leaned over and vomited into her lap.

At last Sarah's stomach stopped heaving. She sank weakly against the tree, her shakes fading, as hopelessness and despair deadened her mind.

Loud shouts near the fort roused her. John and three other settlers were scuffling outside the open gate. Then the others dragged John, kicking and struggling, inside the safety of the palisade.

Stay where it's safe, Sarah thought, as the gate slammed behind them. *Stay where it's safe.* Relief flooded through her when she realized what would have happened if the others hadn't kept John in the fort.

Near her tree, a curl of smoke rose from the Davidsons' and soon became a dragon gnawing away the roof and licking at the walls with a red-hot tongue. The wind shifted. Smoke stung Sarah's eyes, tears streaked her cheeks.

She groaned, picturing Jane, Walter, Margaret, Twig, lying dead inside the burning walls. Then she remembered Twig had gone into the forest before the killing began, and she said a prayer for his safety and for the souls of Margaret, of Walter, of Jane.

At that moment Margaret stumbled through the palisade gate and ran toward the gully, her hair undone, her clothing ripped. Hope jolted Sarah upright. But then Rawhunt and Camohan chased after Margaret and caught her, only a whisper away from the tree where Sarah sat. With one hand thrust about Margaret's throat and the other holding her wrists behind her, Rawhunt forced her to her knees, her head back, her back bowed.

Then Camohan, standing behind her with Jane's long, yellow scalp at his waist, grasped his knife and began slicing away Margaret's hair.

Sarah screamed. So sickened was she by the sight of a living person being scalped—and a person dear to her besides—so sickened, she no longer cared for her own safety. She, too, longed for death, for she doubted she could live at peace with this new memory.

For a brief moment it seemed her scream had gone unnoticed among all the others. Then Rawhunt lifted his head and looked up to where she sat in the tree, her tears runneling down her face, her body numb and shaking with terror. For a moment Indian eyes met English eyes, then the edges of Sarah's world went dark. Rawhunt stood in a circle surrounded by shadow. The encircling shadow widened; Rawhunt grew smaller until he was a tiny pinprick in the gloom.

"Rawhunt," Sarah whispered, just before she fainted. "You were my friend."

Chapter 28

The sun had nearly reached the treetops when Sarah roused from her faint, scarcely believing she still lived, that her shawl still held her safely in the tree. Her eyes closed, she listened, but heard no screams. Then, her heart thudding, she looked down to where she had last seen Margaret and the Indians. No one was there.

Smoke still billowed about the settlement. The company compound, the company barn, most of the houses were smoking rubble. Part of the church still stood. Richard's new house seemed untouched, as did the fort.

Sarah looked into the distance. Thin spirals of smoke curled into the sky downriver at Mulberry Island, upriver at Archer's Hope, across the river at Hogg Island and Lawne's Plantation. *The treachery was well done,* she thought.

The only English people in sight were the few inside the fort, standing on the earthen platform behind its palisade walls. Every few minutes one of them would fire at an Indian that came within range, but for the most part the natives paid the defenders no heed, so busy were they sorting through their plunder and hacking up the bodies of the dead. They had tied Master

Boys's body to the tree in his palisade yard. Sarah recognized him by his shredded green dowlas shirt, for only his torso remained.

A circle of Indians near the Company compound parted to reveal some captives, including Master Jackson's wife Ann. A few other settlers, mostly children, were crowded around her, but their faces were so smudged with soot, dirt, and tears Sarah couldn't tell who they were, or if Twig was among them. They were soon led away, disappearing into the forest with their captors.

The sun was well past midday when, at last, all the Indians melted back into the forest. Sarah stayed in the maple, her head throbbing, her legs numb, her throat parched, heedless of the passing hours, her mind blazing with dancing pictures of horror. At last, her thoughts became still, her eyes shut, and she dozed.

Voices woke her. The palisade gate of the fort swung open, and five men marched out, muskets ready, their leader William Harwood at the head of the column.

With her right hand, Sarah pried open the clenched fingers of her left hand, which still stubbornly clutched a branch. With quivering arms, she untied her shawl from the tree and forced her numb legs to creep down from branch to branch, afraid of what she might find at the bottom, for she could see no sign of Margaret. Her legs wobbled and could scarcely hold her when she reached the ground and looked about.

Margaret was not there. Perhaps she was among those whose body parts lay scattered around the settlement. Shivering, Sarah crept toward the gully and the men on the other side.

She halted at the far side of the gully, within the shelter of the trees, and looked to see if any stray Indian still lurked about. A squaw, the first she had seen, knelt over a body that had fallen near some heavy bushes.

The way the woman moved, the angles of her body, seemed familiar. Sarah froze, not daring to draw a breath for fear she would be discovered. But the squaw was too busy wrenching a ring off the finger of the dead man to notice Sarah. At last the woman held up the ring to examine it, and Sarah saw her profile.

"Rose!"

Rose turned, a knife in her hand. "You!"

"What . . . what are you doing?"

Rose shrugged. "Lookin' out for myself." It was clear the timid, downtrodden Rose was gone; the brazen Rose was back.

"You're dressed like an Indian." Sarah's voice rose in disbelief.

Rose nodded. "I have found where I belong. The Injuns are my people now."

The realization of what this meant washed over Sarah like a cold wave. "You're one of them!" Sarah's gaze shifted to the body that lay behind Rose. Beside it, a spring violet drifted in a pool of darkened blood.

"I did no killing," Rose said, seeing where Sarah looked.

Sarah wasn't certain she believed her. Gathering up her filthy skirts, Sarah edged away. "May the Lord have mercy on you, Rose Howe."

"Oh, he's shown me much mercy already, for I watched with my own eyes as Jacob Howe lost his flesh, strip by strip." Rose threw back her head and gave a silent laugh.

At that moment Sarah heard the men shifting about in the Company compound. She opened her mouth to call out, but a savage movement of Rose's knife stopped her.

"Call out and it'll be the last sound you make in this hell on earth."

Sarah fled.

All thoughts of Rose vanished from Sarah's mind when she burst into the small group of men in the compound, for they were just tipping Richard's body into a shallow grave. His forehead was split, and the blood had flowed into his open eyes and clotted. His mouth gaped wide, as though he still called Anne's name.

John softly cried out, as though he thought Sarah a ghost, and stepped quickly to her side, turning her away from Richard.

"He was right," she whispered, comforted slightly by the touch of John's hand on her shoulder. "And we scorned him for his fears and mocked when he went about in his armor."

"Aye," answered John. "Yet he didn't wear it when he needed it most."

Sarah knew why Richard had not taken time to don at least his helmet. He had been hurrying to Anne. Love had made him human after all.

A few other survivors crept from their hiding places to join them. Some sobbed quietly. Some wailed and rolled their eyes, shouting incoherent words. Some were silent, their faces drawn, their eyes blank, as though unseeing eyes would banish remembered horrors from their minds.

Sarah went frantically to each one, asking, "Have you seen Anne Mills? Have you seen Anne—or Twig?"

"We'll count the dead in the town today," Harwood said then. "If all is quiet, tomorrow we will check for survivors in the outlying dwellings, though I fear there's small hope." He then sent Sarah and the two other surviving women back to the fort.

From the fort, Sarah watched as John and the other men crept from smoking rubble to smoking rubble, though the ruins were still too hot to enter. At times they bent and scooped into sacks the hacked off arms, legs, and heads of those who had not been left in the houses to burn. The few bodies that had not been dismembered or burned were also gathered together. Graves were dug near the remains of the Boyses' dwelling and the dead given a hasty burial.

Because it was too near the fort for the Indians to safely set it on fire, Richard's house was the only dwelling still standing. At last the men entered it, to emerge moments later with the foodstuffs Richard and Anne had gathered.

Sarah hurried to the gate as the men returned. Her throat dry, her tongue swollen into a sour mass, she looked at John, her eyes making a silent appeal.

John shook his head. "There is . . . no hope," he whispered, his voice breaking, the scar vivid on his pale cheek. "I pray they died quickly, for I fear they were all in the house when it burned—Walter, Margaret, Twig, Jane."

Tears squeezed from Sarah's eyes as she shook her head. "Not Twig. He had gone into the forest, so there is still hope for him. And not Margaret. She was not in the house when . . . when . . . Rawhunt . . ." She couldn't go on.

"Rawhunt?" John's voice rose in disbelief. "I cannot believe he played a part in this."

Sarah nodded. "Camohan too. And . . . and Rose." Sarah explained how she had survived and where she last saw Margaret, though nausea rose in her throat as she spoke, the bloody scene danced again before her burning eyes, and she felt overwhelmed with shame that she had not called out a warning to Richard and perhaps saved his life.

John leaned his forehead against the platform wall. "Rawhunt was like a brother to me. It seems I didn't know or understand him at all." He groaned. "How could my friend betray me?"

Sarah had no answer to give him.

At last John raised his head. The golden flecks had faded from his eyes. "Tomorrow we'll look for Margaret. This day is done, and it would be foolish to be out after dusk."

A sob tore Sarah's throat.

John took her hand in his. "People have survived a scalping," he said gently. "I promise we will look again tomorrow. And for Anne also. If we don't find them, perhaps it's because they were taken captive."

Harwood called them together then. "Of nearly one hundred people in Martin's Hundred, only eighteen of us are here in this fort, and we don't know if any other white people are alive in all of Virginia." He wiped his mouth with the back of his hand. The hand shook, Sarah noted, as Harwood continued. "It would be foolish to seek safety at another settlement, not knowing if any survived, so we will stay here and try to endure as best we can. If others still live, let them come to us." Clasping his shaking hands together, Harwood pressed them against his chin. "Now let us kneel and thank God we are, indeed, alive, and pray for those people who dwell away from the settlement, pray that they, too, live and draw breath."

Sarah knelt and prayed fervently for those gathered, for any lost survivor in the forest of Virginia, for the souls of those who had died, but most fervently for Margaret, for Twig, for Anne and her unborn child. But she could not ask God's forgiveness for those who had been her friends, but were now her enemies, not even for Rawhunt, who had let her live.

Chapter 29

The next day the Indians returned, wandering through the settlement and up and down the river, so the men did not search for Margaret or for Anne. Instead, for two weeks the survivors huddled like mice within the fort.

For the first three days, survivors crept out of the forest, telling tales so gruesome Sarah covered her ears as they spoke. Yet some came with no tales to tell. On Easter Sunday Thomas and Matilda Jones and their two sons, who lived scarcely a mile away, arrived at the settlement expecting to attend Easter services, having heard nothing of the massacre.

Sarah spent much of her time walking the platform beside the palisade wall. From there she watched Indians stalk the forest, watched hoping to see Anne and Twig emerge from the greening woods. She scanned the river for sight of an English boat carrying English folk, wondering if any other English were still alive in Virginia and if they'd come before the fort's meager supply of corn and root vegetables ran out.

One day, as Sarah wandered aimlessly past the well toward Harwood's house in the center of the fort, where many of the survivors slept, a shout drew her to the platform. Shading her eyes, Sarah saw a shallop filled with men beach on the shore. At first she thought they were Indians, but then the sun glinted off helmeted heads and plated bodies, and she knew they were English. A column formed and marched toward the fort, a familiar, bearded figure in the lead.

"It's Captain Pierce from Jamestown!" Sarah cried, gripping the planks of the palisade, her face wet with tears. "It's Captain Pierce!"

John appeared beside Sarah. "Perhaps Jamestown survived."

Jamestown had survived, the captain told them, and thanks to an Indian at that. At Pace's Paine, a plantation across the river from Jamestown, an Indian named Chanco had warned Richard Pace of the coming attack. Pace rowed the three miles to Jamestown and gave warning, saving the town.

Other settlements were not so lucky, and it was feared the death toll would go over three hundred. But no settlement had yet reported as many lost as Martin's Hundred, where seventy-eight had died or were missing.

"We have lost six of our councilors," Captain Pierce went on. His composure seemed about to crumble, but he drew himself up, and asked Harwood, "Have you seen to all your dead?"

"No, some still lie in the burned-out houses or are missing. Because the Indians come and go as they please, we haven't been able to leave the fort."

The captain nodded. "After we have accounted for all the settlers, we are to gather what food we can find and return with all survivors to Jamestown. A few plantations are to be left occupied, but Martin's Hundred isn't one of them."

That afternoon the men of the fort went at last out of its walls to search through the rubble of the houses. Long shadows were creeping across the forest floor when they returned. Sarah had watched anxiously from the palisade, and knowing they had been to the Davidsons', hurried to John.

"Tell me," she urged, for John seemed reluctant to say what they'd found. "Tell me. Knowledge is better than the pain of uncertainty. Otherwise, Margaret will stay a fresh wound in my heart."

John took a deep breath. "Margaret dragged herself to the trash pit near the gully. She looked as though . . . as though she had simply gone to sleep." He closed his eyes as if trying to shut out the memory of what he had seen. "She was lying on her side, one arm to her head, the other across her chest, her fingers folded. She might have tried to hide, because I don't think the scalping killed her. I think it was the cold March night. She found her own grave," he finished. "We simply filled it in."

Sarah groaned. "Then if we had found her that first day, she might still be alive."

John looked at her fiercely. "But would she want to be? She was a proud woman."

Sarah thought of Margaret, who believed herself a fortress against the wilderness, who took time each morning to wind her hair into an elaborate roll as if she thought civilization would end if she did not make the effort and, instead, simply twisted it into a knot upon her neck. She pictured that good lady, daughter of a wealthy yeoman, drifting into death in a trash-filled hole, lying amid the ashes, the pieces of broken pipkin, a few rotted pumpkin rinds, old tenterhooks, broken pipes, some slop water.

Suddenly it seemed almost funny, and Sarah began to giggle, then laugh, until her voice spiraled like a clarion into the evening air, and tears streamed down her cheeks like the water down the nearby gully. Then, at last, her face crumpled, her tears of laughter turned to tears of loss, and she wept for Margaret Davidson, who had met her end in a trash pit.

A fine rain was falling the next morning as the column of men trudged away from the fort to search the outlying dwellings. Along with their muskets, they carried shovels and spades, for it was thought only the dead awaited them.

All day Sarah wandered listlessly around the fort, unable to settle to any work, though there was little work to do outside of grinding corn. The cows, Daisy and Whiteface, were dead, so there was no butter to churn. There was no garden to plant, no field to hoe. Even had it been safe to venture outside the fort and into the nearby fields, most of the seed had burned. What little they found, they needed for food.

Sarah had chewed her fingernails till they bled before the men appeared from the forest to the north, no doubt having marched all the way around to the Staples' land five miles in that direction. She raced to the gate and waited with fluttering heart for news of who had lived and who had died.

The men entered, bearing over their shoulders a few sacks of peas, a few barrels of corn. There was no sign of Anne's flaming hair or Twig's unruly thatch in their midst.

Sarah looked at John, his skin drawn tight across his cheekbones and along his beard-shadowed jawline. She knew from his lowered head, from the droop of his shoulders, that they had found no one alive in all of Martin's Hundred.

A cold chill trickled through her. Her fears had now come true. Anne was dead. Twig too. Sarah thought of the baby that Anne would have borne in the summer, the season of *cohattayough.* She thrust the Indian name from her mind, her body filling with rage and hate.

Never again would she use a word from their language. Never again would she greet them kindly, trade with them, share a meal with them. They had taken from her nearly everyone in Virginia—nearly everyone in the world—she cared about.

Not waiting to hear what Captain Pierce had to report, Sarah crept away to the shed adjoining Harwood's house. There she found a pile of sacks tossed into a corner. She lay down on them and curled herself into a tight ball, not caring if she ever rose again.

John found her there as night was settling its shadows over the ruins of Wolstenholme Towne. He lowered himself beside her, then reached out and gently touched her shoulder. "Sarah?" His voice and his touch brought out the thoughts she had managed to hold at bay.

"I should have been with Anne!" she cried. "I should have been with her. But, instead, I thought how nice it would be to spend time sitting in a tree. A tree! And then, when the killing started, I . . . I stayed in the tree." Sarah pounded her fist into the sacks. "I should have gone back to her. If I'd been there I could have . . . helped. I could have . . ."

"You would have been killed—scalped and mutilated just like Anne." John sounded angry. "How would that have helped her?" He reached out, took her by the shoulders and gave her a shake. "Don't blame yourself about Anne. With or without you there, the Indians would have killed her. This way, they had one less victim—and I have one less friend to mourn."

Sarah didn't notice how John's voice broke, for his words had done their job. Her anger turned away from herself, toward the Indians. "I hate them all!" she snarled. "The Paspaheghs, the Chickahominies, the Kecoughtans, the Weyanokes, the Arrowhatocks. I hate all the Indians of Virginia."

"And how do you think the natives of Virginia feel toward the white man?" John asked, his voice quiet.

But Sarah took no note of his question.

"I hate them! I hate them! I hate them!" she continued. On and on she ranted, while the black cloak of night settled around them and wrapped them in its folds.

Finally, exhausted, Sarah fell silent. John had said nothing for a time. Then he asked again, "And how do you think the natives of Virginia feel toward the white man?"

"Surely they must hold great hatred for us too, to have done such a terrible deed."

"And why would they feel that way?"

After a silence, Sarah spoke. "I don't know. I tried to be a friend to the natives I knew. Though in the beginning I feared them, I came to respect their ways, to learn from them. I tried to follow your example, for you were a true friend to the Indians." John gave a soft grunt of pain at her words.

"But the people who sneered at the native ways," Sarah continued, "the ones who distrusted them and called them savages, who didn't welcome them into their homes or feed them at their board, it's plain *they* were the ones who truly saw into the heart of the Indians and knew the treachery there."

"People such as Richard Kean," John said. "People who believe the land won't be safe for the English until all the Indians lie dead."

John smacked his hand into the sacks on which they sat, momentarily silencing the rustling of the mice that had come with the night. "Yet even those others such as you and I—people who respect the ways of the natives—we, too, have earned their hatred. And a well-deserved hatred it is." The bitterness in John's voice was so thick it almost felt like a wave washing outward from John to Sarah, pushing her backward with its power.

"What do you mean?"

When John spoke again, the bitterness was replaced by sorrow. "It's a wonderful dream we have—to build a new world. But building a new world is like preparing a new field to plant. First the forest must be cleared before the crops can be sown. And as the fields spread, the trees are pushed back and back from the land where once their roots grew deep.

"Can't you see, Sarah?" John asked, his voice full of pain and sadness. "We are the new fields. The Indians are the trees."

At last she understood. "We have . . ." She paused, searching for the words. "We have thrust them from their land. We have dispossessed the Indians."

"Yes." Even in the dark, Sarah could sense the vigorous nodding of John's head. "We have taken from them the land God gave them. So they rose up against us and tried to take back what was their own."

"Then they shall have it!" Sarah cried. "It is a cruel, heartless land, and I hate it even as I hate those who would take it back. I'll have to begin again, but as soon as I earn my fare, I'll go home to England, just as I'd always planned."

To her surprise, John chuckled softly. "I think not. I think Virginia is in your soul, and you love it as much as Rawhunt and Camohan do, would fight for it the same way."

Sarah thought about his words. Were not the Indians like the Britons who fought against the hordes of European invaders so many centuries ago? *Had I lived in England in those lost days,* wondered Sarah, *wouldn't I have struggled for my homeland as bravely, as fiercely, even as treacherously, as did the Indians, who see their land being taken from them?*

She thought about her Virginia land, the land that had soaked up every drop of sweat she had dripped onto it, then rewarded her with full, lush tobacco plants. *Wouldn't I fight for this land should someone try to take it from me?* She knew the answer. She would. Indeed she would.

Though the newborn hatred Sarah harbored for the Indians wouldn't fade for a long time, into her heart crept a glimmer of understanding, a compassionate sense of what the Indians must have felt in their own hearts and minds. She leaned her head against John's chest and began to weep.

Chapter 30

U nable to sleep that night, Sarah wandered the platform of the palisade, aching for Anne, mourning
Twig, her saucy stick of a friend so full of banter and
spunk. His body had not been found, so Sarah could
only imagine what horrors he had endured.

The moon silvered the river and the tender spring
leaves. *If only,* Sarah thought, *I were like the leaves
bursting forth with such fresh hope, with no worry
about what lies ahead and no sorrow for what has gone
behind, living each moment as though there were no
other.*

Lost in thought, Sarah looked toward the forest just
as a shadow slipped from behind a tree and glided
toward the heap of rubble that had been the longhouse.
It disappeared, then reappeared almost immediately,
crouch-running toward Richard's house.

Sarah opened her mouth to shout a warning, for none
of the watch had seen the intruder, but something held
her quiet. No harm would come, she told herself, from
waiting until she knew for certain the stealthy one was
the enemy. There was little harm he could do outside
the palisade.

At that moment the trespasser darted from behind the

house and ran toward the fort. Sarah's breath caught in her throat, and hope twined itself about her heart, for there was something familiar about the scampering figure, the way its arms and legs flailed as it ran, the way it cocked its head.

Afraid to utter a sound in case it broke the spell and the vision disappeared, Sarah scrambled down the ladder from the platform and ran toward the gate in the palisade wall. Not waiting for permission from the guard, she flung open the gate just as the figure raised a fist to pound against it.

"Twig!"

Without a word, Twig flung himself into Sarah's arms. He felt like a bundle of the sticks for which he was named as she held him close, for he was thinner than ever.

"Oh, Twig! I thought I had lost you, too," Sarah cried, rejoicing, when moments before she had mourned.

Twig sniffled loudly, then pushed himself away and drew himself upright, as the guard swung the gate shut. "No mum. You cannot get rid of Twig so easy, though for a time I thought it was the end of me, I did."

Sarah studied him. Twig's face and arms were a mass of scratches, his clothes filthy rags; his hair looked like a littered bird's nest. She pulled him to her again. He squirmed and tried to break free, but at last gave in and allowed her another hug.

Taking him by the hand, she led him toward Harwood's dwelling. "I imagine you have a story to tell, but first let's try to find you a morsel of food to feed that scrawny body."

They woke the entire fort that night, but Sarah wouldn't let Twig tell his tale until he ate his fill of suppawn—porridge made from corn flour and water.

"Caught me at the turkey pen, Nayohan did," Twig

said, when he was fed. "Trussed me up and left me there till near dusk. When he came back he had all these bloody hanks o' hair hangin' off hisself, so I knew something terrible had been goin' on. Course I'd been smellin' smoke all day too, but I thought someone was burnin' stumps nearby. But when I saw those scalps, I knew."

"Where did he take you?" someone asked.

Twig shrugged. "To his village, downriver and inland some ways. 'Twasn't a bad place, 'cept I had ta do all the cursed work."

"Were there other captives in the village?" Harwood asked.

Twig shook his head. "I was the only one; leastways I never saw any others."

"So how did you escape?"

"Took me fishin' on the river, he did. I had it all figured to jump overboard and swim ashore, 'cuz I heard Injuns can't swim."

John chuckled quietly when Twig said that.

"But then I saw he meant to tie me in the cursed boat. So I didn't giv'im the chance. Started a brabble with 'im, I did, and got clean away."

Sarah stared at Twig in amazement. "But how could you have struggled with an Indian and still gotten away? He must have been much stronger than you."

Twig grinned, and it was such a triumphant, happy grin, Sarah again wanted to reach out and hug him to her. "I tangled 'im up in the net, I did, and then I did ta Nayohan's finger what Baggie Willie did ta mine," Twig explained, holding up his left hand with its missing little finger.

The gathered crowd cheered.

"After that 'twas easy. Just followed the river upstream till I saw the fort. Took a coupla days though, 'cuz I had ta be careful the sots didn't nab me again."

"So you bit off his finger," marveled John.

At that, Twig began to search through his tattered pockets. "Saved it, I did. Thought you'd like ta see it, since some folk wouldn't trust the word of a beggar brat." He looked around the crowd as though searching for someone in particular.

"Richard is dead," Sarah told him quietly. He looked at her, more questions in his gray eyes. She answered his look. "And Anne. Walter, too. And Margaret. What you see before you are all who survived."

Large tears shimmered in Twig's eyes, but they didn't spill. "They was good ta me," was all he said.

The following day they all sailed to Jamestown. It was an easy move, for there were few provisions to take with them, and most of the survivors, including Sarah, had lost all their personal belongings. Her gray dress now hung from her in tatters, but she looked no worse than the others.

At Jamestown, John and Twig were sent to the company compound. Sarah again went to stay with the Pierces—for how long she didn't know. No plans were made to immediately reoccupy Martin's Hundred, especially after news came that the Indians had burned the abandoned fort.

By July, the air on Jamestown peninsula felt fetid and heavy, and the summer sickness had begun to take its toll on the people crowded behind the palisade walls.

That month, too, the *Seaflower* sailed for England, carrying news of the massacre. The *Discovery* also sailed, carrying John Pory back to England, for Christopher Davison had long since come to replace him as secretary. Sarah missed Pory's round figure hurrying about Jamestown. He was the one person who could smile when all about were weeping. A wink of his eye, and somehow she knew she could make it through another day.

One evening, when the Pierces were off visiting, Sarah and John sat quietly by the fire, listening to the loud voices of songsters echoing around the fort:

*"Bold worthy Sir George Yeardley commander
chief was made,
'Cause fourteen years, and more, he hath within
this country stayed.
Against the King Opechancanough, against this
savage foe,
Did he with many an English heart for just revenge thus go."*

It was now October, and the song was popular among the folk at Jamestown, because former governor Yeardley was preparing to lead an expedition against the Indians. It wasn't the first campaign against them. Soon after the uprising, Treasurer George Sandys led men against the Tappahatonaks, Governor Wyatt against the Weyanokes, Captain William Powell against the Chickahominies, and Captain John West against the Powhatans. But this was to be the most important expedition, for unless Yeardley could capture corn from the Indians, there would be hunger in Jamestown that winter.

"How many men will be going with Yeardley tomorrow?" Sarah asked.

John poked at the fire, scattering sparks. "He has said five hundred."

In the days since the massacre, John had become Sarah's dearest friend in Virginia, bringing her comfort and what little joy she found in those sad times. Now she told him, "So many. I'm glad you're not one of them."

John didn't answer, but rose from his stool and retrieved a bundle from outside the door, which Sarah recognized as his tools, the same tools he had carried with him into the fort the day of the massacre.

"Will you keep these for me, Sarah? If I don't return, will you give them to Twig?"

"Don't return from where?" Sarah asked, her heart fluttering.

"I *am* going with Yeardley."

A shudder passed through Sarah. "But you're needed in Jamestown! There are many houses that need repair and others waiting to be built. Every month new people arrive who have no place to stay."

John's voice was bitter. "Don't you think I would prefer to stay here? I've no desire to become a soldier and go about killing those who were once my friends, to take their corn, so that we will live and they will die. But even though Master Boys is dead, for three more months I'm a servant of the Virginia Company and do as I'm bid." He handed her the bundle.

She took it from him, but her outward calm hid the turmoil inside her, for the thought that she might never see him again once the men sailed away sent her into a near panic.

As she set down the bundle, Sarah kept her back to John so he could not see the fear she knew was in her eyes.

"Take care while I'm away," John said. "I don't know what . . . what would happen to me should I lose you, too. And watch out for Twig. He is worked so hard, he can scarcely keep his eyes open past the evening meal. I think he longs for the days when he had only Walter and Margaret ordering him about." John tried to chuckle, but it was more a croak.

Sarah tried to smooth her ragged breaths. "Come back safely. Twig . . . and . . . and I . . . will miss you."

188

She was about to turn and face him, thinking she might have courage enough to hug her friend farewell, when she felt a cold draft on her neck. When she turned, John had left her.

∞∞

Chapter 31

Five long weeks had passed since the expedition sailed downriver. All that time Sarah went around with a knot of fear in her stomach.

In mid-November, word came with the returning wounded that the Company had driven out the Nansemonds and Warraskoyacks, burnt their houses, and taken their crops. They had then gone to Kecoughtan, up the Pamunkey River to Chescheack, and on to Werowacomoco, the chief seat of Opechancanough himself, where they did the same.

"With more new people arriving every month, we'll certainly welcome that Indian corn," said Mistress Pierce, whose husband was also with Wyatt. "I only wish the Virginia Company would send food with the newcomers." She gave her white head a vigorous shake. "We're forced to feed more and more people with scarcely enough food to feed a few."

One gray November day, during which the rain fell to further dampen Sarah's low spirits, a shout went up that the boats of the expedition were sighted.

Sarah scarcely breathed as the first men came ashore, their armor gleaming wetly. Some of the men were wounded, some ill, but most seemed unharmed by their skirmishes with the Indians and began handing baskets of corn ashore to eager folk waiting to carry it to the storehouse. She saw no sign of John.

Twig appeared at Sarah's side. She shook her head, silently answering his unvoiced question. With a frown, Twig tugged at a hank of his hair.

Rain trickled coldly down their necks and oozed into their shoes, as they watched Mistress Pierce welcome her husband. Sarah was tempted to ask the captain if anything had happened to John, but she feared her throat was too tight to speak, for she was beginning to think he was dead.

Two men came ashore, hefting between them another who had one leg bandaged and dragging behind, whose face was masked by scruffy whiskers. Twig jabbed Sarah with an elbow. "It's John!" He ran toward his friend, then stopped and turned back to look at Sarah, his eyebrows crumpled. "You! Why are ya standin' there with yer mouth agawp? Come on!" And he ran back to grab Sarah's hand and drag her after him.

Sarah's legs had turned to water from the relief of seeing John alive, but now strength surged through her as she flew with Twig toward John, her feet hardly touching the ground as they dodged among the people, leaped the puddles, and darted between baskets of corn waiting to be carried to the storehouse. As they reached him, Sarah had time only to notice how glittering John's eyes seemed, how flushed his cheeks, before his head dropped forward and his body sagged.

The two men holding John laid him on the soggy ground. "What happened?" Twig asked, helping Sarah shelter John from the drizzle with her cloak.

"It was at our last raid." The older man who answered sported a ragged, grizzled beard that appeared to have been trimmed with a knife. "Thought all the savages had fled, we did. Then one sprang on us as we started back to the boat with baskets of corn. John knocked him down, but the Indian whacked John on the leg with his hatchet. Hit him with the poll, else the leg would have a wicked wound. As was, the bone broke. Has a fever now, too.''

"Would you carry him to the Pierces'?" Sarah asked, hoping the couple would let her care for John there.

As she watched the men drag the limp form of her friend toward the fort, Sarah felt once again the small kernel of fear she'd known while John was gone.

"Many times I've cursed my armor," stated Captain Pierce later that day, "especially during our raids in the heat of last summer. But this time it was right welcome." He slapped his knee. "The arrows simply bounced off, so not many of our men were killed. Course, the Indians moved faster than we could, so we didn't kill as many of them as we have in the past. But a few paid for the wickedness they wrought last spring."

Sarah sat next to John, bathing his brow with a cool rag as he slept. The Pierces had agreed to let him recover at their home, and he now lay on a pallet next to the fire. He had been delirious when they pulled on the leg to set it, and while Mistress Pierce made it fast with hickory strips and bound it in clean linen. Now, though he still slept, his fever had finally broken, and Sarah's fear had begun to dissolve.

The captain had been describing the expedition, but now he emptied his pipe into the fireplace and rose to his feet, yawning. But before he took himself to bed, he laid a gnarled hand on Sarah's shoulder. "He's a strong lad, and youth is on his side," he told her. "And if the love of a woman counts for anything, I think young Clark will be clambering about on roofs again soon after Yuletide."

"I think I'll have Dr. Pott come tomorrow to check his leg, nevertheless," Sarah said.

It wasn't until the Pierces had retreated to their corner of the house that Sarah realized what the captain had said. Her face grew as warm as the flames in the fireplace. *The love of a woman? Why, the captain thinks I'm in love with John.*

Sarah looked down at John's pallid face with a smile, thinking she would have to assure the captain that she and John were only dear friends, when her breath suddenly caught in her throat. She felt as though a ray of sunlight had peeped over the dawn horizon after the blackest of nights. Clasping her hands over her mouth, so she wouldn't cry out in amazement, she thought: *The captain is right. Dear God, the captain is right.*

For a long time Sarah sat beside John, trying to decide when she had first begun to love him, trying to decide what this knowledge would mean, how it would change her life. *How I wish Anne were beside me to share her advice,* she thought, sorrow for her dead friend mixing with her newfound sense of joy.

At last Sarah decided that loving John would not alter her life, except inside her, where no one could see. She had changed a lot from the timid girl who had arrived in Virginia more than two years before, but she was not brave enough to tell John how she felt, especially not knowing if he felt the same.

It has been nearly a year since John told Margaret he would think about taking me for a wife, Sarah told herself. *And although it has been a year of sorrow and misery, surely, if he wanted me for his wife, he would have spoken to me before now. So I'll keep my feelings hidden.*

Hesitantly Sarah reached out. Her hand shook as she brushed John's dark hair from his forehead. He stirred, but didn't awaken, merely smiled a wisp of a smile, and slept on.

Through December, as John's leg began to heal, Sarah managed to keep her feelings secret. Luckily there were other things to keep everyone's mind occupied. Three ships had arrived within the past month, each carrying something on board to set tongues wagging. The *Truelove* carried supplies for one of the abandoned plantations, which Governor Wyatt appropriated for the people of Jamestown.

The *James* caused the most uproar; it carried the first orders from the Company since word of the massacre had been received in London.

"They're blaming *us* for the massacre," roared Captain Pierce, when he had heard what the Company wrote, and returned home to report to his wife. "Said we didn't take enough precautions against the Indians."

Sarah could imagine Richard nodding his head over that accusation.

"But that's not all," the captain continued. "Among other things, the Company says we also invited the massacre because we wear clothing that is too fancy and drink too much strong drink!"

For a moment there was a shocked silence. Then Sarah looked down at her rag of a gown, thought of the foul water they drank, and started to laugh. Soon the Pierces and John joined her.

When the laughter had quieted, the captain muttered, "They're sending four hundred men in the spring, but, of course, the Company can send no food. So, once again, we must feed them as well as ourselves."

"At least the one hundred fifty new settlers who came on the *Abigail* brought enough provisions to last them for a time," said Mistress Pierce with a grateful sigh.

Her husband snorted. "Don't forget the governor's wife was on board. Had it not been for Lady Wyatt sailing on the *Abigail*, I've no doubt the ship would have carried only its passengers and their diseases." He tugged at his mustache. "At least Lady Wyatt seems to have escaped the ship's sickness, which I've heard caused many dead passengers to be thrown overboard."

"Aye," said Mistress Pierce. "I've heard the sickness was caused by the *Abigail's* beer, which stank so, people could not stay on deck because of it."

The captain then announced the news that caused John and Sarah to look at each other with hopeful eyes. "The abandoned plantations are to be replanted as soon as possible." The older man nodded at John. "Martin's Hundred included. Lieutenant Parkinson, who came on the *Abigail*, is to replace Lieutenant Kean, but I don't know how soon he and his men will travel to Wolstenholme Towne."

"What about the Indians?" Mistress Pierce's voice rose, the way it always did when she worried about someone's safety.

"They won't be any problem," the captain reassured her. "As many have been killed since the massacre as died since the colony was seated in 1607." He shook his head. "Besides, the Company ordered us to exterminate any still alive."

John's groan filled the room. "Not more killing."

Captain Pierce shrugged. "I'm afraid so. Rewards are even offered, an especially fine one for whoever captures or kills Opechancanough himself. The children are to be made into servants." He sighed and shook his head again. "Better the little ones should be left in peace. That order will only give us more mouths to feed."

Sarah felt sickened by the news, especially about the children. Even if they weren't taken as servants, they would probably die, since their parents were to be killed.

Later, she told John, "Once Richard said there would be no peace in Virginia until all the natives were dead. It seems his words have come to pass."

"And a sad day it is," John added, shifting to a more comfortable position on his bench. His leg was healing well, the color had returned to his face, and the yellow flecks again glinted in his eyes. "When Lieutenant Parkinson sails to Martin's Hundred, I plan to sail with him." He looked at Sarah. "I hope you plan to go, too."

She was bubbling with joy, but Sarah only nodded.

Chapter 32

By December 1622, nine months after the massacre, as many settlers had died from illness and starvation as had been killed in the attack. And by the end of January 1623, the disease that arrived on the *Abigail* was rapidly adding to that number. No one knew what sickness it was, for the animals were dying, too.

Few people died in bed. They were taken so quickly they fell on the ground and lay there like rotten sheep, as full of maggots as they could hold, until the few who were well could bury them.

One evening, as Sarah frowned at her small portion of peas, water-gruel, and bread, she announced, "It's time to find Lieutenant Parkinson and ask when he's going to Martin's Hundred and if we can return with him. I'll go tomorrow."

"I'll go with you."

Sarah shook her head at John. "No. You don't have all your strength back. It's better if you stay here and not tempt the sickness to visit you, too."

For a moment John's shoulders slumped, then rose again. "If the sickness did take me, at least I would die a free man," he announced proudly, for only that month his indenture had ended.

The next afternoon Sarah hurried from the home of Captain Powell, where Lieutenant Parkinson was staying. She held a handkerchief to her face to mask the stench of the dead and dying, but her thoughts were happy ones. The lieutenant had agreed that in eight days she, John, and Twig could return with him to Martin's Hundred.

She was nearing the church when she heard a loud shouting at the gate. From the scattered words echoing around the fort, Sarah soon learned two Indians were approaching under a banner of truce. When she saw the natives—the first she had seen close up since that bloody day last March—her stomach churned, her skin prickled, her hair rose on her arms. When Sarah saw one of the Indians full-face, a faintness clutched at her, and her vision narrowed until the world stood as small as a pinprick. Camohan! She had last seen him drawing his knife against Margaret's scalp.

As the Indians were led away to the Governor's Mansion, the blackness faded from Sarah's vision, and she hurried home.

"They came from Powhatan's brother, Opitchapan," Captain Pierce told them later that evening, his spiky eyebrows lowering and the crease between them deepening. "They want to settle at Pamunkey and their former sites again. In return, they'll free the captives they've held since the massacre, and we would be permitted to resettle our hundreds in peace."

"Will the governor agree?" said John, from where he sat propped on a stool near the fire.

Captain Pierce shook his head. "Who can say? Robert Poole is in favor of the treaty. He believes if the Indians free our people and begin to feel secure again, it will be easier to surprise them and cut down their corn, since we'll know where they plant. Otherwise, they'll plant in hidden fields, and it might be impossible to find their crops.''

"That's a heartless reason to agree to the treaty," snorted Mistress Pierce.

"It is," agreed her husband. "But I suspect the governor may do just that if it means the return of those poor souls who have lived so many months with the heathens."

"And what . . . of the two Indians?" Sarah's voice quavered. "Have they already returned to their chief?"

"Likely they will be sent back tomorrow, after the governor has made his decision," answered Captain Pierce.

"Not Camohan!" Sarah blurted, making a small, gagging sound when she spoke the man's name. She felt sorrow over the plight of the Indians and even understood why they had treated the settlers so cruelly, but the memory of what Camohan did to Margaret and the thought of him going free sickened her.

"Why this concern about Camohan?" asked Captain Pierce.

The dark thoughts in Sarah's head froze her tongue to stillness, so John spoke for her. "Camohan was an actor in the massacre at Wolstenholme Towne. Sarah saw him scalp Margaret Davidson."

Mistress Pierce gasped, and the captain growled deep in his throat. "The other native who came, Chanco, is a good Indian," he said. "The people of Jamestown owe him our lives. But I think perhaps Opitchapan laughs in our faces by sending to us this Camohan, who has taken the lives of our friends and loved ones." His voice broke, and he reached out a hand to his wife, no doubt thinking of their son Thomas, their daughter-in-law, and their grandchild, who had died at Mulberry Island. Mistress Pierce dabbed at her eyes.

"This Indian must not go free," vowed Captain Pierce, and he stomped out of the house.

The next morning Chanco was sent back to his chief with word the English would accept the treaty offered. That afternoon Camohan went on trial for the murder of English settlers.

Afterward, Captain Pierce told Sarah that Camohan refused to make a statement when the governor questioned him, giving no sign he understood the questions, though he spoke English quite well. Sarah was called soon after to give her testimony.

Sarah was the only woman in the church where the proceedings took place, since women were discouraged from going into court unless they were on trial. When she was called to give her testimoney, the thought of speaking before so many strange men made her bones rattle and her breath come in shallow gasps. Only the sight of a few friendly faces among the jurymen—and the memory of Margaret—kept her from fleeing.

Her heart turned as she spoke, for she could feel Camohan's dark eyes staring at her. She haltingly told the court how she had seen him take Margaret's scalp, how she had recognized Jane's yellow curls hanging at his waist. When she finished, her stomach was quivering. She didn't know if it was from relief that her moment in the public eye was over, from the ordeal of remembering that heartrending day in March, or from knowing her words might send a man to his death. She hardened herself against the latter. *Perhaps my heart has become calloused,* she thought, *but I want Camohan to die.*

"Is Mistress Douglas the only witness?" asked Sir Yeardley, who was acting, rather half-heartedly Sarah thought, for the defense. "Must I remind the court that serious cases need two witnesses?"

Later, Sarah told herself the devil must have seized

her tongue, for even though Sir Yeardley had not addressed his question to her, she surprised herself and spoke again, her voice trembling. "Of course there are no other witnesses. All others who may have seen Camohan that day are—dead."

A murmur passed throughout the room. "The circumstances in this case are unusual," said Governor Wyatt then. "I don't believe a second witness will be necessary."

Sir Yeardley didn't argue the point, and moments later Sarah was dismissed, though she longed to stay and hear the verdict.

"The jury found the Indian guilty," Captain Pierce told them. "He is to be hanged tomorrow. You know, he never so much as twitched a muscle when he was sentenced." The captain shook his head and went to fetch his tobacco.

At noon the following day, a staccato drum roll sounded through the fort and brought everyone who was not sick or dying out of doors.

"They're going to execute the Indian," someone shouted. Sarah felt repulsion at the thought of seeing a hanging, but her curiosity was even stronger and drew her toward the gathering crowd. "Stay here with me," John called, but Sarah went on her way until she stood beside the gallows.

Camohan stood on a cart in Gallows Swamp, his hands tied behind him, his head raised proudly, his face free of expression. When the captain asked if he wished to be heard before he was hanged, he again gave no sign he understood. With that, the captain gave a signal, and the cart was pulled from beneath Camohan's feet.

It was a gruesome way to die. He had seemed indifferent beforehand, but when he dropped, Camohan began to twitch and jerk, as though trying to keep the rope from tightening.

Sarah didn't turn away as the man bucked at the end of the rope. He was a large man and did not die quickly, so the captain signaled again, and another man hung on Camohan's legs to hasten his death. Even then, it took two or three minutes before his strangling was done.

Sarah marveled that she could watch with such a cold heart, marveled she did not cry out for mercy for the man whose people she claimed to care about. Yet she soon realized why she stood silent. Although she felt an understanding for the Indians of Virginia as a people, for Camohan she felt nothing more than hatred, the hatred she would feel for any man who murdered her friend, no matter his race. Deep in her heart, she had been longing for revenge.

As Camohan spun slowly in the winter breeze, this thirst was quenched, and the black pool of hatred that stood in the pit of Sarah's stomach drained away. A feeling of peace took its place. At last she turned and walked home through the freezing puddles, satisfied that that day justice had been served. Anne, Margaret, Walter, Richard. All were avenged.

But as she helped prepare the evening meal, Sarah remembered it was she who had sent Camohan to his death. If she hadn't asked after him, Captain Pierce wouldn't have known Camohan played a part in the killings at Martin's Hundred. Then her testimony wouldn't have been heard. Pain pricked at her conscience, and she silently prayed that God would forgive her for her part in that sorrowful drama.

∽∽∽
Chapter 33

Two days later, Mistress Pierce banished John to the company compound with Twig. "That leg has healed enough for you to get around, and those prisoners the Indians've held will be returning any day now," she said. " 'Spect one of them will bide with us, so you must be gone."

"Bet you'll be right glad to get away from that dithering Mistress Pierce," teased Twig, when he came to help carry John's few belongings to the compound.

John threw back his head and gave a snort of laughter. "Lucky you are the lady in question is outside planning her garden and can't hear your rude remarks."

Twig glanced around at the timbered house. "S'pose this *is* better'n the compound, what with all the sickly blokes lyin' about there."

Sarah handed Twig the bundle of tools John had put into her keeping three months earlier, before he sailed downriver. "Thank goodness it's only for two nights."

Twig grinned at her, the old familiar grin he had given her the first day they'd met. "Yup. In two days it's home again." He pulled a face. "Then I s'pose it'll be back to hoein', hoein', hoein' and weedin', weedin', weedin'."

Sarah thought of the land waiting for her downriver, its tobacco hills warting empty and brown from the soil. She sighed an immense sigh. "Oh, I hope so."

"I hope so, too." John handed Sarah the crutch he had carved. "I won't be using this anymore. Time to strengthen this leg if I'm going to hoe, hoe, hoe and weed, weed, weed the fifty acres I get as my freedom dues." His face was so full of joy it was all Sarah could do to keep from throwing her arms around him. She looked down, afraid her feelings were awash in her eyes.

Twig gave Sarah and John a sharp look. "Yer not gonna spend the whole night whimperin' 'bout how much ya miss this place and Sarah, are ya? Cuz, if so, I'd rather sleep with the cows."

There was silence for the beat of a heart, as John's gaze met Sarah's and locked there. Her breath caught, waiting for him to speak. Then John shook his head, chuckled, and gave Twig a push out the door. "Get a move on or I'll give you a little finger on your right hand to match the one on your left," he told the boy, and limped after him.

Sarah watched them go, filled with womanly disappointment—and girlish relief—that John hadn't answered Twig's question.

The next day Chanco reappeared, bringing not the twenty or so captives the governor hoped for, but only one, Mistress Boyse, whom Sarah didn't know. Thinking, no doubt, that the English would be less provoked if the single freed captive seemed well-treated, the Indians had dressed Mistress Boyse as a queen—but as an Indian queen, not an English queen, an act that would have hardened the settlers' hearts even more against the Indians, had it not been for Mistress Boyse herself.

Around her middle the woman wore a deerskin apron. Her limbs were adorned with copper beads, her upper body painted red with bloodroot. But, except for a handsome mantle of turkey feathers over her shoulders, she was naked above the waist. But the woman did little to hide her nakedness. She walked boldly through the gate of the fort as if she were, indeed, a queen, bearing herself regally, heedless of the shocked stares, the averted glances, the angry muttering of the crowd. Although Sarah was dismayed by the sight of the woman's shameful state, her heart swelled with admiration when Mistress Boyse passed so proudly.

From out of the crowd, Mistress Pierce appeared with a cloak, and invited the freed woman to her home. That evening, after Mistress Boyse returned from meeting with the governor, she described all that had happened to her and why she was the only prisoner set free.

"The other prisoners weren't returned because Chanco overheard some threatening speeches made by a Mister Poole. It seemed Poole wished to use the treaty as a way to further subdue the Indians and take their crops." Mistress Boyse held her hands out to the fire and sighed contentedly.

"I knew Poole spoke too freely," exclaimed Captain Pierce, smacking a fist into his palm.

"Tell us about the other captives," said Mistress Pierce, and Mistress Boyse listed off the names she remembered.

Sarah jolted upright when she heard the name Ann. "Ann? Ann who?"

"Ann Jackson," replied Mistress Boyse, and Sarah sank back onto her stool, remembering Mistress Jackson, John Jackson's wife, who had been marched away with the captured children. For a moment she had dared to hope. But no, her Anne was dead.

"It was strange, though," Mistress Boyse said, when she finished listing names, "that when we arrived at the Indian village there was already a white woman living among the natives. She wasn't a prisoner. She'd come there of her own will for reasons she didn't wish to speak of. She seemed a haunted person. Dark she was, with a lean, hungry look about her.''

"Rose," Sarah murmured.

After Sarah described Rose's life and how Rose had fled Martin's Hundred, then returned to loot the bodies after the massacre, Mistress Boyse gave a shake of her head and a click of her tongue. " 'Twould indeed seem to be this Rose. But I believe the life of an Indian suits her. She has even taken a Paspahegh brave for a husband and has borne him a child.''

"Poor wee babe," Sarah breathed.

"No," answered Mistress Boyse. "The Indians hold their children dear, and no harm will come to *that* infant.''

As Sarah went off to prepare for her last night of sleep in Jamestown, she looked at the hearth where John used to lie and thought of Rose sleeping somewhere in the forest with her Indian husband and her baby. And Sarah felt something she never thought she'd feel when she thought of Rose—a twinge of envy.

When Sarah woke in the early dusk of the new morning, she felt so odd she thought she might cry, for it was the day she was to leave the foul stench of Jamestown and return to Wolstenholme Towne. She was returning to a burned-out waste of a town, to days of hunger and hard work, but she was happy to be going back.

When it was safe, she could even live on her own land, because, finally, a Thomas Nicholls was surveying and marking out boundaries in Martin's Hundred. It might mean making soap ashes again, but Sarah was determined to find the fee of six shillings a day to pay the man to survey her land, so she could receive her title.

For a moment sadness overwhelmed her at the thought of going back to a settlement where there was no Anne, no Cisly, no Margaret or Walter to encourage her, at the thought of working her land alone when . . .

"No use dwelling on what might have been," Aunt Mary's voice echoed from the past. Sarah shook her head, forbidding herself any regretful thoughts. With Walter and Margaret dead, she told herself, perhaps she could convince Harwood to let her have Twig for a servant. With Twig to help, she wouldn't be alone, and she could accomplish a lot more.

Feeling more eager than she had for months, Sarah scrambled out of bed. It took her only minutes to pack her bundle, for all she owned were a few gowns she had acquired from the belongings of the newcomers who had died. The two chests she had carried to Martin's Hundred two years before, and which she had thought so meager, now seemed a fortune.

Sarah was sitting down with the Pierces and Mistress Boyse to a meal of water-gruel when John arrived, a worried look on his face. "I must speak with you, Sarah," he said, beckoning her outside.

"What is it? Has Lieutenant Parkinson changed his mind? Is Twig ill?"

John shook his head. "No, no. But there's something important we have to do before we sail downriver. Already it's been left too long, but I've been reluctant to broach the subject." He frowned and rubbed an earlobe. "It seemed a small matter compared to the misery and want surrounding us. But it can't be put off any longer."

Sarah's heart pounded, afraid John had something dreadful to tell her, his look was so serious.

"Sarah," he said, "before we sail downriver to Martin's Hundred, I'm asking you to become my wife."

The mist that rose in tatters from the ground like wraiths from an open grave seemed to dance behind Sarah's eyes. Then a flush mounted into her cheeks, a sudden shyness overtook her, and she couldn't meet John's gaze.

It was the moment she had waited for, longed for, ever since John's return. Now she stood, struck dumb.

"Don't play coy with me, Sarah," John scolded. "Even though I was not yet a free man, I was a fool not to mention that I . . . I have come to love you, and to hope we would be married when I gained my freedom." He straightened himself on his good leg and squared his shoulders. "Besides, you have no choice. Already the governor's brother, Reverend Wyatt, is on his way to the church. I told him and some others that my bride and I would meet them there in a few minutes. If you don't give me your promise at once, I shall be forced to march next door and ask the Widow Emerson to wed with me instead, else I won't be able to hold up my head among my fellows."

At that Sarah's shyness vanished. Laughter bubbled out of her, because the Widow Emerson was a wizened, toothless old woman who looked like a shriveled pumpkin.

"Oh, yes! I will be your wife."

Suddenly the day seemed different. Each dried leaf, each clod of dirt on the street, each thrusting, brittle cornstalk stood out of the fog with great clarity. The fetid water smelled more pungent, the drifting smoke more biting. The thwack of an ax sounded sharper, the cry of the goose more haunting.

John gave Sarah a shy kiss. "I fear I will make a rather tattered bridegroom." He spread his arms wide to show his ragged shirt and breeches, his threadbare coat.

"We shall be the perfect match," Sarah reassured him, spreading her tattered skirts, in turn. "Come." She led him indoors.

The Pierces and Mistress Boyse were finishing their meal, but when John and Sarah entered, Mistress Pierce looked up with a twinkle in her eyes. "I think the young folk have some good words for us."

"Leave the chores," John ordered. "You're going to a wedding."

Reverend Wyatt was waiting at the church when they arrived, along with Lieutenant Parkinson, Twig, and a few others. And Sarah sensed the approving presence of her mother, father, and aunt, of Margaret and Walter, Cisly and Anne, even that of Richard and Hannah.

Twig nudged Sarah with a bony elbow and grinned. "I always thought John Clark was the one fer ya."

"You rascal." Sarah nudged him back.

John's voice and hands shook as they exchanged vows, but when it was over and they walked from the church as husband and wife, he was his calm, steady self once again.

Outside, the sun shone, and the rime that had fallen during the night glistened so, Sarah's eyes were dazzled, and she felt she walked in a dreamworld. But the man at her side was real, and the hand encircling her own was warm and comforting.

The rising February sun warmed the earth and wreathed it with curls of vapor that swirled about them as they walked toward the yet fog-enshrouded river and the boat waiting there to carry them to Martin's Hundred. Even the sight of the burial party going about its gruesome task didn't steal the serenity from Sarah's morning.

At last, Lieutenant Parkinson, Twig, John, and Sarah were on board with the others who were waiting. With waves and cries of farewell, the boat pulled away from the shore and struck out for the middle of the James. The sail thrust hopefully upward into the mist, which clung to Sarah's face and mingled with her tears of joy. As those waving from shore faded into that shifting veil, the sun broke through, and they sailed on down the river in a haze of gold.

ᗣᗧᗣ

Author's Note

The lost settlement of Martin's Hundred, founded in 1619, was inadvertently discovered by archaeologists in the 1970s, when excavations were undertaken at Carter's Grove, Virginia. An attempt has been made to depict the physical characteristics of Martin's Hundred as accurately as possible, based upon the findings of those archaeological excavations.

Although many of the incidents in *Sarah on Her Own* are fictional, some are based on actual events. Young women and orphans did go to Virginia from England on the ships named around the time depicted, the women to become wives to the unmarried settlers, the orphans to become servants.

The Indian uprising of March 22, 1622, is a documented occurrence in which approximately 347 settlers died, seventy-eight of them at Martin's Hundred. The events of the massacre have been described as accurately as possible.

Just as many incidents described in the book are based on truth, so, too, are many of the people who walk through these pages. Richard Kean was the chief lieutenant of Martin's Hundred. It is known that he lost his life in the uprising, but it is not known for certain how he died, although a skeleton was found in the Company compound. According to archaeologists, it belonged to a tall, muscular man with a well-developed wrist, typical of a swordsman. The author has taken the liberty of claiming this unknown skeleton as Richard Kean.

While Margaret Davidson is a fictional person, another skeleton—a woman's—was found in a trash pit near a homesite. This skeleton showed evidence that the person had survived a scalping and possibly died in the pit of exposure.

The Pierces, John Pory, Governors Yeardley and Wyatt, Samuel Maycock, John Rolfe, Edward Sharpless, and many others named in this book lived in Virginia during the time the story occurred. William Harwood was the leader of Martin's Hundred, John Jackson and John Boys its first burgesses.

The Indian Chanco is credited with having saved Jamestown from the uprising. Camohan played a part in the killings at Martin's Hundred and later was executed for his deeds. Mistress Boyse was held a prisoner by the Indians at Pamunkey and later returned "apparelled like an Indian Queen." An Ann Jackson, variously described as the sister or wife of John Jackson, was held captive by the Indians for about six years. Upon her release, she returned to England.

After the uprising, Martin's Hundred apparently was resettled, but it never attained a prominent position in early Virginia, and eventually settled into the dust of history.

If you enjoyed *Sarah on Her Own*,

sample the following brief selection from

PLAINSONG FOR CAITLIN,

the next historical adventure in

American Dreams,

coming in April 1996 from Avon Flare.

On the first of April, my sister, Rebecca, broke her big news. She waited until Molly, our housekeeper, was off to market, then drew me into the parlor and sat me down in the rocker. She sat on the crewel-covered stool at my feet and spread her skirts around her.

"I have a plan for our future, Caitlin. It is the best of news for us," she told me.

"Oh, your news is finally ripe for picking, is it?" I teased, then caught my breath. Beneath the quiet surface of her face, she looked like a well about to bubble over. I watched on edge as she fished a packet of letters out of her pocket. They were tied up with one of her blue hair ribbons, and the envelopes were addressed in a bold, clear hand. She held the packet in her hands a moment before she went on.

"Yes. My news is ready for telling now—and everything is working out better than in my wildest dreams. Caitlin, do you remember Emma Everett?"

I stopped rocking in my chair and nodded. "The Cortlands' servant girl." I racked my brain for a moment. Emma had attended the same church as us. She was a pleasant young woman who would have been pretty if not for her pockmarked face. "What in the world does Emma Everett have to do with us?"

"Remember how she went West?"

"Right!" I clapped my hands together. "How could I forget?" Emma's departure from our circle of acquaintances in New Bedford had created quite a stir, though for the life of me I couldn't recall the details.

"She answered an ad in the *Sentinel*," Rebecca said.

"To be a housekeeper?"

Rebecca took a deep breath. "To be a wife."

"To someone she'd never met?" I asked, but suddenly the small scandal Emma caused came rushing back to me. There had been some cruel talk about how a girl as homely as Emma needed to answer a stranger's ad to find a man willing to marry her. I hadn't paid attention to the marrying part at the time. I just thought it was terribly exciting to set out on a new life out West, where land was cheap and plentiful and gold filled the hills and streams.

"Well, I saw such an ad, quite by accident, about two months ago," Rebecca went on. "And I decided to answer it."

I gaped at Rebecca. "You answered an advertisement? In the newspaper? To wed a stranger?" I jumped up, nearly upsetting the rocking chair. "Someone we don't know? Who isn't from New Bedford? After you wouldn't let me wed Henry Gare, you are going to marry a perfect stranger? Have you lost your mind, Rebecca?"

Rebecca looked up at me a moment, then shook her head. "It's not the same thing as Henry Gare and you."

I scoffed, "It certainly isn't! He is a friend. We know him. Our father trusted him enough to make him our guardian. . . . He won't let you do this. I'm sure he won't."

"He won't have a choice. He was our guardian only until I came of age. I am now twenty-one."

I put my hands to my face. Of course. Rebecca's birthday last month had been nearly forgotten in all our grief about Pa and Ethan. I stared down at her and shook my head in disbelief.

Rebecca got up and went to the window. Leaning against the pane, she looked out at the brown yard with its patches of old snow and fresh purple crocuses.

"How, after Ethan, could you marry someone you have never met, let alone don't love?" I demanded.

Rebecca's shoulders stiffened. She faced me. "Caitlin. About Ethan. I have known a most wonderful love, and I will never be able to love a man that way again. But I am young, and I want to wed, and I think I can fashion a new life for us."

"Us?"

"I would like you to come with me out West, to Nebraska."

"To live with you and this man you have not even met? In Nebraska?" My dreams of the West had more to do with Colorado mining towns or the hills of Oregon. All I knew about Nebraska was that the transcontinental railroad went clear across it, through Omaha. It did not sound like someplace I would like to live—let alone Rebecca, who was far more delicate.

"No, I haven't met him in person," she said quietly. "There's no chance to. He cannot leave his homestead to come to New Bedford. But we have exchanged letters, and I think I will like him, and maybe even grow to love him. I don't know that. If we meet and feel we aren't fit for each other, then I will either come back here, or perhaps fashion a life for us in Omaha, or Lincoln, or move to San Francisco."

I couldn't believe it was my quiet sister Rebecca speaking. I didn't even know how to argue with her about this. Rebecca leave New Bedford? Except for the marrying part, answering an ad to move to the frontier sounded like something I might do, but not Rebecca.

"You don't even know what he looks like," I pointed out.

Rebecca bit her lip and blushed slightly. "Oh yes, I do. It is not a good likeness; the image is blurred. But here—" She picked up the bundle of letters she had put on the carpet and pulled a small daguerreotype from an envelope. It showed three roughly-dressed men leaning on picks and shovels beside some railroad tracks. One wore a Union uniform from the war. The image was blurred, as Rebecca said, but I saw they were all smiling and seemed so eager, so confident, as if no hardship were big enough to touch them. Rebecca touched my sleeve and shyly pointed to one of them. He wore no uniform and was taller than the others. His face was blurrier than the rest.

"That's him," she said. "That's Nathaniel Briscomb. He calls himself Nate."